A LETTER OF MURDER

A SEABREEZE BOOKSHOP COZY MYSTERY BOOK 2

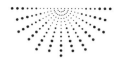

PENNY BROOKE

CHAPTER ONE

J handed Melba Reece a coupon—five percent off any title, new releases not excluded. I nodded toward the table in the front marked *New and Intriguing Finds.* "See the big red book in the middle? It features small-town beauty queens, corrupt cops, and family drama. Right away, I thought of you."

Who Killed Marianne? was not my kind of book at all. But I knew my customers; I knew them very well, and Melba loved true crime.

Let me introduce myself. My name is Rue, and I match those who come to me—seekers of knowledge and adventure—with the perfect read. And it is my fervent hope that they find true love here at my gran's carefully curated store, the Seabreeze Bookshop. While she's beginning her dream retirement, I'm living the dream here in Somerset Harbor, Massachusetts.

Melba blushed, as if she were a teen and not the middle-aged proprietor of the local sandwich shop. "I know you have to wonder why I read the stuff I do," she told me in a quiet voice as she picked up the book. "But I like the little peeks into other people's lives. And all the clues they give you? Well, it's kind of like a puzzle. You have to understand that I am in no way *gleeful* that these people died. Oh, you know what I mean." She turned the book over in her hand and read the blurb on the back.

"I don't judge," I said. "The classics sections is no different. Those authors over there are always killing someone."

I glanced down at the envelope she'd pushed into my hands when she'd first come in. It was part of a new promotion: in exchange for a family letter (if it was vintage, all the better) for my friend Elizabeth's new book, customers received a coupon. Elizabeth, my best friend, operated a small business in the corner of my store with old scrapbooks, postcards, and other treasures from the past. I loved how our business interests fit so well together; we were both, after all, essentially the same. There were stories to be found in both sections of the store.

Of all the things she sold, Elizabeth found the most

fascination in old letters, and now she was putting a book together to benefit the Literacy Foundation of Southeastern Massachusetts. It would be filled with saved and treasured letters from the families here in town.

Melba saw me looking. "You can read it if you like," she said. "It's to my mother from a friend. Dated 1945. And it has a recipe for—you won't believe it, Rue—a white *sangria* salad. You should write it down! With grapes and pineapple juice and I don't know what." She picked up another book. "Oh! And there's a lot about her two sons going off to World War Two—both of them left the same week. Does that not make your heart stop? I just can't imagine."

Another local named Allie Lane walked toward us. "Ooh, I'd love to see it." As always, she looked striking. White-blonde hair curls fell across her shoulders, and her blue eyes always seemed to be full of fun—and perhaps a little mischief. Now, she smiled at Melba. "Sangria in the Jell-O, huh? That sounds like a party." Allie came in almost once a week to browse through the cookbook section, which was really funny, since she didn't cook. But she'd gaze at the color pictures of desserts with the kind of wonder that I saw more often in the section on world travel.

My golden retriever woke up from his nap and

barked a happy greeting. Allie grinned and knelt down to rub behind his ears. "Gatsby! My good boy!" she cooed.

"Come by the shop today." Melba looked up from her book to acknowledge Allie. "The special is crab salad, which I know you always like. And we have some good corn chowder. I've decided that I'll make it now with a little added kick."

"Oh, I should try to get away and have some," Allie told her. "The store always gets so crazy before the holidays." She owned Elegant Furnishings on Main, an airy shop where soft music and cheese biscuits on the counter made the fine fabrics and gleaming mahogany of the merchandise seem even more appealing. The hallmark of the store was sophistication, but always with an Allie touch. On one particularly comfy-looking sofa, she had left a sign: "We must add a surcharge if you decide to take a nap." And when I'd had a children's author in to read her book, *Little Goose Gets Lost,* Allie had hidden tiny geese toys all around her store for the kids to find. "Send them across the street once the reading's done," she had said to me. Of course, it was a plan designed to encourage sales, but I had no doubt she'd done it for the kids as well. There was a part of Allie that was still a kid at heart.

"I can imagine that it's busy at this time of year," said

Melba with a sigh. "When you know company is coming, that's when you see how old and really *sad* your old brown sofa's looking. Or that the guestroom's looking worn. I'm just happy *our* Thanksgiving will be at my sister's house."

Allie grinned. "You did *not* hear this from me, but vases of fresh flowers all around the house make the best impression if you're expecting guests. Of course, that little tip would be terrible for business. So please do me a favor and keep that to yourselves."

We laughed as Allie handed me a letter for Elizabeth's collection. "It was with my mother's stuff. It was kind of nice to dig out her old boxes from my closet. Kind of like a little visit with my mom." A sadness fell across her face, and my heart went out to her. Allie had lost her mother when she was a teen. The two of them had been close, from what I understood.

Allie pushed a stray curl from her eyes. "My mom saved everything, you know? Like wedding magazines from way back in the day. And the fabric samples from the gowns that her bridesmaids wore back in 1990! That pink almost was florescent. It could make a person blind." Her eyes went from bright to melancholy. "And here she could have planned another wedding. She'd have been all over that."

Melba caught my eye, and my heart kind of sunk.

Allie had a wedding of her own that she was in the midst of planning—with no mother of the bride.

"But I think Elizabeth will like my mother's letter." Allie perked up a little at the thought. "I can't wait for you to see." She opened the envelope. "She wrote it to her father when she was a little girl."

I glanced down at the childish scrawl, which was, in essence, a long list of candy bars, which had been ranked by taste. Young Catherine Lane had added in some recipes for two confections of her own creation. And there were crayoned drawings of pink bears enjoying the treats.

"There it is again—that pink," Allie told me wryly.

"What a treasure," I said, smoothing out the page. "Elizabeth will love it." I knew Elizabeth was especially eager to get letters that had links to our local history. And Allie's family was well known across the country as the longtime owners of Something Sweet Confections. Allie's great grandfather had grown the business into the nation's top-grossing manufacturer of candy bars. That now included the iconic Cathy's Crispy Nougat, named after Allie's mother.

"Oh! And look what else I found with her stuff. I absolutely love it!" Allie reached into her purse and pulled out a small box, opening it to show a blue crystal bird. "I'm taking it to the store to keep it on my desk." It was beautiful and delicate, very finely made. Most likely, I decided, this was an expensive piece. Catherine Carrington Lane—and all the Carringtons—had always had the money to afford the best.

"My mother always had a thing for bluebirds, although I don't know why. So this just kind of seems like a little piece of her." Allie wrapped it back up carefully and put it in her purse. "She always told me, 'Allie, when you see a bluebird, that means things will be okay.' So this might be my sign. It's still so hard without her, even after all these years."

Catherine Lane had gone to bed one night at the age of fifty-six and never woken up. The cops said that she'd been poisoned. But despite wild speculations in the tabloids and the TV news about who had killed the heiress, no real suspect had emerged.

"She'd have been thrilled about the wedding," I said, trying to focus Allie's thoughts on the good things ahead. "Tell me, do you have your dress?" With Allie's mother gone, I worried for the girl, kind of like an older sister might. Allie was like me. She knew a lot about a lot of things; she was very capable, but the simplest of things tended to escape her mind. More than once, she'd paid me for a book and dashed out of the store without it.

I hoped that by now she'd booked the florist. They

got booked up so quickly! And it would be like Allie to wake up on the morning of the wedding and suddenly decide that flowers would be nice. Again, she was like me—which made me worry for her more.

But Allie didn't answer as she stared out the window. Then suddenly she startled, as if emerging from a trance. "Oh sorry, Rue. So sorry! It's just been a real bad week. Ever since I heard about Elizabeth and her book with the letters, I've spent a lot of time reading through my mother's stuff. We told each other everything. Or at least I thought we did. So I was so surprised that... Oh, don't mind me. I'm rambling!" She pushed a curl behind her ear.

"Would you like to talk about it?" I asked her carefully.

"Maybe, but not now. I've just found out some stuff I have to process for a while."

"I understand," I said. "Next week, let's do lunch. You know I want to hear every single wedding detail. Oh, and here's your coupon." I handed it to her.

"Next week." Allie smiled as she took her coupon and headed toward the cookbooks.

But there was to be no lunch. The next week she was dead.

Allie went to bed one night and did not wake up.

Like mother, like daughter, I thought when I was told about what happened. Wasn't that the saying?

The news spread quickly through the square in urgent whispers; the news was analyzed in somber huddles as the town took on a mournful air. What had happened to our Allie? She'd been young—just twenty-four—and seemingly so healthy, always on the move. The girl had been so energetic that she rarely even slowed down to a walk, it seemed.

Then more news quickly followed. Homicide, the cops said—homicide by poison.

Like mother, like daughter, I thought, which, now that I thought about it, was one of those old sayings that I could do without.

CHAPTER TWO

I texted my friend Andy: *Come by after work for drinks?* I could have used a chardonnay, and I had the perfect big front porch for cocktails. But mostly I was desperate to get some information. Andy had been a cop forever here in town. Now he was retired, taking on some odd jobs as a private eye, but he still helped the local cops when something big was up. Which was a real good thing, because Andy had a good mind, and the police chief was...well, *clueless* was the way to politely put it.

His reply came right away. *I won't say no to a drink. But you know I have to keep a lid on what's going on with the investigation.*

Hmm. I was only hoping for a *tiny* clue. But, really, nothing he could say could make me feel any better.

They could arrest someone right away, but that would not bring Allie back.

Uncannily, I'd lost *another* friend to murder just the year before, and the pain from that one still felt fresh. Somerset Harbor was not a town you'd associate with murder. It was a place for charming shops and old-world charm, where cobblestone streets were lit the old-fashioned way—with gas lamps. The crime statistics here were low, which was one of the many reasons that tourists came in droves to the Harbor, which is what the locals called our town.

Another text came in from Andy. *Did Allie ever speak of a Roger Houston? Or did you ever hear of him? Tall guy with a mustache who's been hanging out in town the last week or so?*

I thought about the question, which took me by surprise. No, Allie had never said a word about him. But I had seen that guy! And he'd given me the creeps. He'd come in a few times, didn't seem too friendly. He'd glanced through some books on local history and then had been on his way. The whole time, he'd just *stared* at everyone around him, like he wanted something from us that we wouldn't want to give.

She never mentioned him, I texted back. *But I've seen him in the store. What's the story with this guy?*

Can't talk about the case.

Why was he such a stickler? I was always telling Andy that he should lighten up. The man wore a tie, for goodness sake, just to watch a show at the Ocean Playhouse, where the town put on a musical each spring as well as a Christmas drama in the winter.

The store was busy that day, mostly filled with local people who were popping in and out of shops to see who might have more details about the investigation. Most thought that Allie's death had to be connected to her mother's—but that had taken place almost nine years before.

Since I was fairly new in town, Elizabeth had filled me in about the theories on the death of Catherine Lane. She told me a little more when we had a break in business. We settled against the comfy cushions of the curtained Book Nook, a place designed to encourage customers to linger with the merchandise.

"Most thought that it was someone after the family money who did away with Catherine." Elizabeth pulled her long gray hair over one shoulder, looking grim.

I picked up my little cat and nuzzled him for comfort. I always felt a little better with Oliver warm against my chest, purring louder than you'd think such a tiny creature could. "Yeah, the Carringtons—they must have been worth a fortune," I told Elizabeth.

"And Catherine was the sole heir. But the bulk of

what she had went to either Allie or charities for children, so if money *was* the motive, someone's plans were foiled."

"Wasn't there a sister?" I vaguely recalled talk of a family scandal, but someone could write a book about the rumors of intrigue that circled around families in the Harbor, many of whom enjoyed some degree of fame—or quite a bit of wealth. I knew that Catherine had lived alone in the family mansion, a massive stucco and stone structure that looked to me like a castle. When I'd come here as a child to visit my grandmother, I would always ask to walk past that house by the sea. I liked to imagine that a princess lived there. Even in those early days, I was a connoisseur of stories.

Once, Gran had taken me to a party there when I was five or six. And our charming hostess Catherine *had* looked like a princess as she'd bent down to offer me a cupcake on a tray. She'd worn a pink lace dress on that night, and she'd had that smile that I later saw on Allie's face—like she knew the kind of secret best shared with a child.

Later, I came to live in Somerset Harbor to run my grandmother's store, and Allie had moved into the stucco "castle" with the water view after her mother's death.

Beside me in the Book Nook, Elizabeth let out a sigh,

nudging my mind back to the present. "Oh my, yes. The sister! You're right. They had *two* daughters—Catherine and Corinne. Now, Corinne, she had her own mind; she was stubborn like her father. And was eventually disowned." She reached down to welcome Gatsby, who had come to settle at her feet. "They were twins, you know."

"Really? Twins?" I asked. "Why was Corinne disowned?"

But before Elizabeth could answer, we were interrupted by the jingle bell I'd hung on the door to announce new guests. Gatsby sprung up to give a joyful welcome to the short, round man who ambled into the room.

"Ed, how are you doing?" I stood up to greet him. "Can I help you find a thriller? Or is it biographies today?" Ed was hard to pinpoint. My book radar sometimes failed me when it came to him. He had lots of time to read since he'd retired from the fire station back in June. And it seemed like the affable grandfather tried a new genre every week, with biographies and thrillers emerging as his favorites.

When he came in for a new book, he'd hit me with a fun fact from his latest read. Because of Ed, I knew that Thomas Jefferson once briefly kept two grizzly bears on the White House lawn. "Caged, of course," Ed had said.

"They were a gift—a big surprise. He didn't keep them long, because how could he keep two bears? But they were quite a hit out there on the lawn for all to see."

Now, I gave him a smile. "What do you know today?" It was my standard question to him, and his answer never failed to make my day.

But today Ed looked dejected. "What I know today is that there are monsters in this world. Who would do such a thing, Rue, to such a sweet young girl? I was just in her store last month—to get a bookshelf. You know, I'm running out of room for books! And she was just delightful, as nice as she could be. You would never guess she came from that kind of money."

"Yes, everyone loved Allie." I looked down at my phone. Another text from Andy.

If Roger Houston comes in, text me right away. Try not to be alone with him, Rue, if you can help it.

I typed a *w* and then *h*, but before I could type a *y* to finish up the word, he sent another text.

You know not to ask. I can't talk about these things. Just be careful, Rue. I mean it.

Well, that sounded ominous. I put down the phone. Andy had been close to my grandmother, and I knew he'd made a promise that he'd look out for me.

A chill ran up my spine. I'd assumed that someone had gone after Allie in particular—most likely for her money. But what was Andy saying? Did Andy have a reason to think that maybe none of us were safe?

Ed wandered over to Elizabeth's corner, where she'd strung a series of vintage letters in celebration of her latest project. Customers loved to stand and read them. Some had been decorated by artists long ago with hand-colored pictures that were quite elaborate. Some were written inside cards with glittery designs, the gorgeous kinds of cards you don't see anymore. I had put a table next to her display with pretty stationery and nice pens. Why should letters be relegated to the past?

I was straightening a line of books when I heard Ed cry out. "Ouch. Hey, I didn't see you there." He maintained his overly polite, always genial way of speaking, but I also heard annoyance in his voice, which was rare for Ed.

I looked up to see a tall man hurriedly brushing past him, not even taking time for an "Excuse me."

My heart skipped a beat. It was the now-infamous Roger Houston. Dressed in a denim shirt and khaki pants, he stared at the letters, frowning, then headed to the local-interest section, where he flipped through some books.

"Welcome to the Seabreeze Bookshop. Can I help you with something?" I forced myself to smile. Beside me, Gatsby growled, and Oliver peered at him worriedly from behind a stack of books.

"No, thank you. No help needed." He didn't take the time to turn and say it face to face. Soon, he was out the door.

"Well, my goodness," said Ed, frowning.

"You've got that right," I said. What was up with this bumbling oddball, spreading his special brand of rudeness all around the square? Had this man killed Allie?

A knot formed in my chest. Whoever poisoned Allie did not deserve to run around and do as he pleased while her life had...stopped. But Catherine's killer was still out there, free—after all these years. And I didn't have much faith in the local cops to catch the person who'd killed Allie.

I remembered the look on her face when she'd told me she was engaged. "I can't wait for you to meet him!" She had grabbed my hand. And in her eyes, I'd seen pure joy, the kind of joy few people feel after about the age of eight—in my experience, at least.

I glanced out the window and saw Roger Houston cross the street. I could hear Andy now, as if he were right beside me, giving me that special look that he saved just for me. *Leave that stuff to us, Rue. You stay right where you are.*

But in the light of day, with people all around, what

could it hurt to follow Houston and see where he went? That might give us a clue and get a killer off the street. Or eliminate a suspect so that the police could focus on the right guy.

There *had* to be a reason that this Houston guy was lurking around the square looking like he was out to throttle everyone he saw. And I had a mind to find out for myself what that reason was.

"Elizabeth," I called out. "Watch the store for just a minute?"

She raised an eyebrow at me. She was just like Andy; she knew me all too well.

"You be careful, Rue," she said.

"Okay, I will," I promised. And I grabbed my coat along with Gatsby's leash.

CHAPTER THREE

O f course, I didn't know if Roger had gone left or right after he'd crossed the street. *Oh, for the love of War and Peace.* And were those raindrops that I felt?

Gatsby pulled me to the left, where he saw a crowd gathered at the front door of the bakery. Gatsby loved a crowd, and crowds usually responded with lots of ear rubs and exclamations about how handsome Gatsby was. Plus, there were always dog treats waiting for all the pets at Anna's Sweet Dreams Bakery. And so we turned left on all our walks if Gatsby got his way.

"Okay, you lead the way," I said. Left was as good a way as any, I supposed.

He slowed down at the bakery, yelping pitifully in protest when I just kept going, past the crowd of people, past the bakery treats. "Sorry, boy. So sorry." But I had to do it; the creep had gotten a head start. We had to move —and fast. "Maybe on our way back," I said to the dog. "If we're not caught in a monsoon." The afternoon had grown dark, and the air felt heavy with the wetness that I sensed was on the way. If I didn't catch sight soon of a denim shirt, a pair of old scuffed boots, and the glaring face of one Roger Houston, I'd have to admit defeat or risk getting drenched.

Then, just past a clump of people waiting for a table at The Crab Shack on the corner, there he was: Roger Houston, stepping out of a tobacco shop and glancing at his phone. I picked up some speed, almost tripping over a discarded cup and running into a light post. Gatsby yelped loudly in surprise when I stepped hard on his foot.

"Whoa, Rue. You okay?" Bill from the barbershop suddenly appeared and reached out to grab my arm.

"Oh yeah. Just, well...clumsy."

"I get it. I've been known to have some run-ins with these posts myself. If they don't watch where they're going, we'll have to lock them up!"

As he laughed loudly at his own joke, I glanced, crestfallen, at the space where Houston had once stood. He'd disappeared again. But right? Or left? I didn't know. It was like a game I didn't want to play. I wasn't good at games.

I tugged on Gatsby's leash, pulling him from the barber, who was rubbing the dog's back. "Great to see you, Bill," I called over my shoulder. "Watch out for those light posts. They will get you every time!"

"Hey, Rue!" Bill called out. Much to my chagrin, he was jogging after me. "There's this book," he said, "that I thought about last week that I'd love to read again. It had a grizzly bear, a pirate, and I think there was a ransom note hidden in—"

"Let me think on that," I interrupted, coming to a stop. "I will let you know. But Bill, I'm really sorry. I'm running very late for a...nail appointment."

He looked confused. "A nail appointment? Really? They let dogs in that place?"

Well, no. No, they didn't. Shoot! I was a lousy liar. "I've made plans for Gatsby to...go hang out with...Ava! You know, at the boutique! That cute little shop next to the nail place. Ava and Gatsby, they're real tight."

He frowned. "I thought Ava was allergic."

"Oh no. Ava, she loves Gatsby. So sorry! Gotta run."

At the corner, I turned right, hoping I was still on Houston's track. The sky was growing darker as I speeded up my pace to a kind of walk-run. And soon, I saw him in the distance, heading into the glass offices of our local TV station, Channel 8.

I was out of breath when I pushed open the heavy doors to step into the lobby. To my left, Houston was asking—or demanding, really—to see Regina Whatley, who was the weather girl.

The receptionist let him know she was not available.

"Not available?" he boomed. "Or do you really mean that she'd prefer to stay behind her desk when a member of the public would like to have a word?"

The receptionist, a redhead with carefully applied heavy makeup, maintained her professional demeanor. "What I *mean,* sir, is that she and our other on-air talent are tied up with preparations for the afternoon newscast."

He turned angrily on his heels and almost collided with me. Gatsby growled at him, and he quickly moved away. Oddly enough, for a man with such a strong build and rough deportment, I think he was scared of dogs.

"May I help you?" asked the redhead, watching me warily as if she were hoping she wouldn't have to deal with two nutjobs in a row.

"Yes! Hello! I...wanted to inquire about..." Again, I was bad at lying. With my heart beating fast, I tried to think of a good reason to be standing there. I thought about proposing that they do a story on Elizabeth and the tales told in the letters that she was collecting. Which was a great idea, but not at that very moment. I had to stay on Houston's trail.

"I am so, so sorry. I think I must have popped into the wrong office space," I said as I backed out the door.

I hurried down the street in time to see my target jump into a black sedan—an Uber, perhaps? *For the love of Marley's ghost,* I thought. *I've surely lost him now.*

Just then, a clap of thunder rang out, and Gatsby began to shake. Gatsby hated storms. This wasn't good at all.

But there was one good thing: a cab was idling at the curb.

"Are pets allowed?" I asked the driver.

"All the same to me," he said.

I jumped in and quickly said, "Follow that Uber just ahead. Me and that guy, we're together."

He raised an eyebrow as he gazed at me in the rearview mirror. I imagined that he sensed a bit of drama in my weird request. How "together" could we be if we couldn't share an Uber? I imagined that he thought I was a stalker, and that thought mortified me. As he pulled out onto the road, he shrugged his shoulders as if to say that a guy sees a lot of crazy stuff when he drives a cab. All the same to him!

The rain began in earnest, complete with loud booms of thunder, and a frightened Gatsby huddled in my lap, his head buried in my shoulder. After a short drive, we pulled into the dirt parking lot of the Eighth Street Café, an all-natural vegetarian restaurant that had been around for ages. The sprawling wooden building was painted a robin's-egg blue, its colors somewhat faded. A porch with a view of the water stretched across the back.

I got out and paid the driver, thankful that the rain had almost stopped.

Inside, Houston was seated near the back and already had a beer along with some chips and guacamole. Since I had Gatsby with me and could only sit outside, the hostess offered to dry off a chair for me. I chose a spot by the door with a good view of my target.

A young waitress soon appeared at my table, looking bored. Her shiny hair was pulled back into a ponytail, and she wore some trendy jewelry to offset the black pants and white shirt that I imagined she was told to wear.

I ordered cola and some carrot ginger bisque. I'd never been to the café, but some of my customers had told me the soup there was outstanding.

Most importantly, the long-suffering Gatsby finally got his treat, delivered by the smiling hostess.

Houston looked as morose as ever, but a round of staffers stopped constantly at his table, some of them even sitting for a while to chat. I'd been under the impression he was a stranger to the Harbor. But people seemed to know him at the café.

"That guy seems popular," I mentioned to my waitress, fishing for a little info when she came with my soup.

"Yeah, I think he used to work here. Like, a long time ago—before I was even born." She added that last part with an air of dismissal—like she saw no need to bother with people and events from that long ago, like youth somehow made her special.

"Can I get you something else?" she asked. I glanced back at my menu, pondering a muffin while she pulled impatiently at her necklace.

"An apple muffin, please," I said.

I enjoyed my soup while keeping a close eye on my target. At times, he seemed to almost crack a smile as he talked to the staff. At other times, the discussions seemed intense, and his anger seemed to deepen beyond his usual I-hate-the-whole-world kind of scowl.

The waitress saw me looking when she came back with my muffin and some butter. She moved a little closer and spoke in a low voice. "Some of the people here? Who've been here a long time? They were all excited when this guy walks in the door. They say he used to be a cool guy way back in the day. But now the man's a jerk. He's always wanting refills, extra napkins, extra sauce. And I bet you anything I get a lousy tip. That's the way it goes; I see his type all the time. I always think *Just shoot me now* when a guy like that walks into my section."

When I called a cab to take me back, the same driver as before circled around in front. He didn't look at all surprised to see that my "companion" was not along for the ride. Thankfully, the rain had held off while I dined al fresco, but it began to fall again as we made our way back to town.

CHAPTER FOUR

*B*ack at the Seabreeze Bookshop, the store was almost empty.

"We were busy for a while," said Elizabeth. "But I think this sudden rain drove the crowd away. I got a little worried, by the way, about you and this furry guy right here." She moved her eyes to Gatsby, who had fallen immediately asleep in his favorite corner.

"Well, you know what I was up to. No need to pretend. Go on and ask your questions."

"I'll make you some tea, and you can tell me all about it," said Elizabeth, heading to the station where we kept the tea supplies. "I'm just glad you're back in one piece."

As I settled into the Book Nook to recount the afternoon's adventure, the rain picked up its pace, pounding hard against the window. With a mug of blueberry tea in hand and Oliver dozing in my lap, a sleepy sense of coziness engulfed me.

First, I told Elizabeth about the TV station.

"He wanted to see the *weather girl?*" She slowly sipped her tea. "Now, that's a mystery for you. I just can't imagine what might be up with that."

"But that gave me an idea. You should call over there and pitch a story on your book."

"You know, I should." She nodded. "I'm glad you thought of that."

"And then he went to that vegetarian restaurant, the Eighth Avenue Café, and Elizabeth, do you know what I heard from the waitress? She said he used to work there —a long, long time ago."

Elizabeth's eyes grew wide. "The Eighth Avenue Café?"

"Yeah, that's where he went. Oh, and let me tell you, our customers are right about the soup. We should have tried it long ago. The soup there is to die for."

Elizabeth looked thoughtful. "*The Eighth Avenue Café.* Oh, Rue, I wonder what it means that he went there."

"There must be something that I'm missing." I put down my mug. "Tell me what you know."

"The Eighth Avenue Café. There's a connection there with Allie's mother." She settled back against the cushion. "As you know, the place has been around forever.

People here have always loved it, but once it almost closed. The expenses were too much. Healthy food, you know, is more expensive to prepare, and that blue building by the water was ancient even then. One repair after another. You know how it goes. But then at the last minute, a wealthy benefactor stepped in for the rescue."

I knew where this was going. "Catherine Lane?" I asked.

She nodded. "At that time, the café was owned in part by Corinne, her sister."

The one who was disowned. "Well, I guess that makes a lot of sense that she would help her sister out," I said.

"Well, yeah, you would think. But not with these two sisters. You see, the thing was, Rue, that Corinne and Catherine hadn't spoken for a while. They hadn't spoken since the rift between the father and Corinne. So everyone was shocked when the news came out that it was Catherine who'd come forward with the money."

"What was the rift about?"

Elizabeth shook her head. "The family kept it private. There aren't a lot of secrets in this town that don't eventually come out, thanks to the busybodies. But this is one of those rare secrets that have stayed within the family." Elizabeth thought it had to do with a controlling father and a daughter who was strong-willed, much more so than her quiet sister. "But if that was all there was, I think that Catherine would have stayed close to her sister. Catherine always did the right thing, Rue. I thought a lot of Catherine."

"When did this all happen, the trouble at the café and the gift from Catherine to her sister?"

"About nine years ago or so."

I let that sink in. "And Catherine must have died soon after that."

"Seems significant."

"And right before *Allie* died, she found out something new related to her mother. Something that seemed to leave her rattled. And now this guy comes back into town. It all seems to fit together—although who knows how." I had already told Elizabeth about Allie's final visit to the store and the things she'd told me then.

"You should go to the cops and tell them all this stuff," said Elizabeth.

"One step ahead of you. Tonight, Andy's coming over." And I had more to tell him than I thought I would when I first sent him the text to say let's have a drink.

"It's a puzzle," Elizabeth said. "But mostly, it's a shame. I just keep thinking about how Allie would have been a lovely bride. She had her whole life before her!" Then she looked me hard in the eye. "Did he see you, Rue? Do you think this Houston guy knew he was being followed? Subtlety, you know, has never been your strong suit. You can stand out in a crowd."

"Hmm. He *was* way ahead of me when I crashed into a light post. That's one good thing, at least."

Things had moved so quickly I'd forgotten to be scared—until that very moment. But I knew what I would do. I had lots of extra beds. I decided that tonight, once Andy had finished with his lecture about me getting too involved in things that might get me killed, I'd ask him to spend the night. Houston might have taken note of me at the TV station and at the café after that. If he put two and two together, who knew what he might do?

I just knew there was no way I'd get any sleep in my gran's big house alone.

CHAPTER FIVE

*T*he sky always saves its best shows for the nights that follow a hard rain. The sunset, with its pinks blending into vibrant reds, helped to still my nerves—as did the chardonnay.

Andy seemed to be on edge as well. "A murder gets more complicated the more prominent the family is. At least that's how it seems," he said as he picked up his glass of gin. He was middle-aged, with a physique that betrayed his appreciation for the fine dessert and seafood offerings in the Harbor. He leaned back in his rocker. "I can't talk about the case, but I know you were fond of Allie, and I can promise you we're on it. And that we've got some leads. I think we've got some good ones."

I hesitated. "As do I."

He watched me, half curious, half wary. It was his opinion that I tended to insert myself too much in the lives of others. "One of these days, your big heart will get you into trouble," is what he'd always said.

Now, he leaned forward in his chair. "Okay, Rue, I'm listening. Tell me what you know."

Rubbing Gatsby's head as he settled in beside me, I began with the conversation that I'd had with Allie the week before she'd died. I told Andy that the victim had found something that disturbed her in some boxes that her mom had left behind.

"Well, just between the two of us, Rue, we believe the killing was related to some things that were going on with the family business. And those things all began *after* Allie's mother's death. So whatever Allie might have seen in those boxes of her mother's, it didn't get her killed."

I was not so sure. "What was happening with the business?" I took a sip of wine.

"Ah, not all was sweet at Something Sweet Confections. All kinds of labor issues and mishandling of money. Not that Allie was involved at all in the running of the place. But if some angry nut wanted to strike out against the person at the top? Well, technically, that's Allie. Because Allie was the heir."

"So it was just coincidence that Allie died the same way as her mother? That's hard to believe."

"Well, maybe not coincidence. The manner in which Catherine died was a well-known fact. So someone with a hatred for the Carringtons might have thought it all a big joke to take the daughter out that way as well. Just to be extra cruel, turn the knife a little more. Sometimes that's how it works."

"I think the two deaths may be connected more than you think they are."

He picked up his glass again and gave me a small smile. "Well, thank you for your input, Sergeant Rue, but there are people who have badges who are on this thing, and in a big way at that. And there are things we know that make us fairly certain that we're on the right track with the investigation."

"You're watching Roger Houston. Andy, tell me why."

"That's confidential, Rue. You know that."

"Okay, okay, I get it. But back to a connection between the family murders: don't you think that Roger Houston links the two of them together?"

"Roger Houston has no known connections to Allie's mother, Rue."

"And that is where you're wrong! The Eighth Street Café, it was once owned by Catherine's sister, from whom she was estranged. And also…it was the place where Roger Houston used to work!"

He stared at me in silence. "And you know this because…"

I hesitated and took in a deep breath, bracing myself for his reaction. "I followed him today."

He closed his eyes and sighed. "Your grandmother made me promise that I would keep you safe. But she didn't tell me you'd go chasing after people who might be a danger—and very possibly connected to a murder." He paused. "But this is interesting. He worked at the café? Do you know when that was? Okay, Rue, you've got my interest." He leaned forward, glass in hand. "Please, Rue, tell me more."

I described my afternoon and the talk I'd had with the waitress. I told him that Houston wanted, for some reason, to connect with the weather girl who worked at Channel 8. That last part seemed to flummox Andy as much as it had me.

"Do you think he'll kill again—whoever it might have been who poisoned Allie?" I asked in a small voice.

"I will tell you, Rue, that there's reason for concern. Yes, we think the act of violence was aimed at Something Sweet, but we also have a reason to believe the anger might have spread to include the whole community who supports the candy maker and takes pride in what they do. So when I tell you to be cautious, that means lock your doors, don't walk alone at night—and if you see Roger Houston, walk the other way as opposed to chasing him. I think that guy's bad news."

"He's unpleasant, surely. But you still haven't said why he's even on your radar."

Rather than respond, he picked up his glass and finished up his gin. I didn't ask again. We both knew the answer: "Confidential information."

"And on the subject of bad-news guys and danger," I said, "I've made up the guest room…if you wouldn't mind."

He grinned. "What kind of breakfast comes with that?"

"Well, mostly I eat oatmeal. Or sometimes a banana. But I'm fairly good with omelets—with the mix-ins of your choice."

"As long as you need me, Rue, you know that I'll be here. In fact, I brought a bag. It occurred to me that it might be the thing to do. You've got a nice place here, but it's kind of isolated. You shouldn't be alone, especially now that I know how you spent the afternoon. Hopefully, he didn't notice that you were watching him."

The company would be nice, I had to admit. I'm fairly introverted, but I was close enough to Andy that I could relax with him, maybe play a hand or two of blackjack after supper in the evenings.

"Thank you so much, Andy. You really are the best."

Gatsby nudged his knee as if to thank him too.

Andy winked at me. "I might let you take your chances if it weren't for Gatsby here, but look at this good dog. How could I not stay and keep him safe?"

And with that, I said goodnight. It had been quite the day.

CHAPTER SIX

The next day, I was looking over orders, considering a new line of coffee table books that featured famous pets. They were the kind of books that could sell very well here, I decided. Those who make their home here seem to love five things most of all: a good dog, a friendly cat, a sunset, an ocean breeze, and a bowl of Melba's creamy, thick clam chowder. (Or perhaps the lemon cake from Anna's Sweet Dreams Bakery. It's quite a town for foodies!)

I was engrossed in the book descriptions when I glanced up to see a tall young man set two books on the counter.

I was instantly intrigued by this stranger in the store. What a quiet, unobtrusive soul this man appeared to be with his expensive-looking khaki coat and his dark lustrous hair that almost reached his shoulders. I hadn't even noticed when he walked in the store.

"I apologize," I told him. "I didn't even greet you or see that you'd come in. But welcome to our store! Did you find everything you need?"

"Oh, yes. Absolutely. You have a nice selection." He nodded in appreciation. "I'd heard this was a great store, and my fiancée was right. I just hoped that I'd come in one day and buy a puzzle book or something—anything but this." He looked down at his selections: *Coping with Deep Loss* and *A Compassionate Companion for the Recently Bereaved.*

I felt a wave of recognition as I saw the dimple in his chin and the way his hair fell into his eyes. Allie had described him with such girlish giddiness. "He's got these dreamy eyes that make you want to melt," she had told me once, "but the guy won't get a haircut till I drag him to the barber. And I'm always saying to him, 'Babe, you need to cut your hair so I can see those eyes!'"

"You must be Allie's Barry," I said to him softly.

"And you must be Rue." He held out his hand. "Allie talked a lot about you, said you knew all there was to know about what books to read."

"We all thought the world of Allie." Then I paused and we stood quietly, listening to the sounds coming from the street. All book people know that words, despite all their power, have their limits too. There were no words that had the proper weight to fit this sad occasion.

I bagged his two selections. Hopefully he'd find some wisdom in the books that would comfort him somehow.

I shook my head and held my hand up when he held out his card. "Consider them a gift," I said, "and come back if you want more."

"That's very kind," he said. "Allie always told me that the Harbor had some amazing people. I've always thought that it was gorgeous, and I could see right away why she loved it like she did. I just got into town and was headed to the inn when I saw your store and thought that I'd duck in."

"Are you at the Abbington?" I asked. It was the nicest place in town.

He nodded. "That's the place. Of course, I guess that there's no reason I can't stay at Allie's like I always do, but that would just be—" He paused to rein in his emotions.

He must have driven in from Boston, where he had a good job—something to do, I thought, with technology. Allie had also said he was searching for work here as he and Allie planned to make their home in Somerset Harbor after they got married.

"If I can do anything for you at all, please just let me

know," I said. "Let me do that—for Allie." We kept a bowl of small chocolates for sale by the cash register, and I slipped a couple into his bag.

As I watched him return his wallet to his pocket, my mind went back to an afternoon last spring when I'd run into Allie at the Somerset Nights Street Fest. She'd been full of wedding plans that day and was expecting Barry to arrive later on that night. "He's just perfect, Rue," she had told me. "I've been dating him for three years, but I still kind of melt when he gives me that big smile." She'd blushed. "You'll see what I mean when you finally get to meet him. And you'll say 'You go, girl. *Your* man, Allie Lane, is the finest of the fine.'"

"I appreciate your kindness." Barry's voice brought my mind back to the present moment. "I'm going in tomorrow to make all of the arrangements, and they'll let everybody know about the service and the time." He took my hand again, and I saw a kindness there—when he should be the one on the receiving end of comfort.

You were right. You did good, I said to Allie in my mind. And it almost broke me that she couldn't hear.

Barry took a deep breath. "You know what?" he said. "Rue, I've changed my mind. I'm thinking now I'd like to stay at Allie's place tonight. Just to be among her things. I think that might help a little, if anything can help. Plus, I have some things to take care of at her place. Like, I have to figure out what she might have wanted me to pick for her to wear when she..." Too choked up to finish, he held his hand up to say goodbye.

I gave him a sad smile. I imagined that the tears glistening on his cheek must match the bit of wetness that I felt on mine.

CHAPTER SEVEN

he rain started up again a few hours later,
which resulted in me having the store to
myself for a good part of the day. I took out my prized
leather notebook (from our Luxurious Musings line—
my favorite) and began to write down all the questions
that I had about the murder.

What was Houston up to? And what did Andy know
about the man that he wasn't saying? Something about
Houston had Andy on alert.

I thought for a moment. But instead of coming up
with theories, I listed even more things I should investi-
gate: What was it that Allie had found in her mother's
boxes that had her so upset? Was that revelation
connected in some way to my sweet friend's murder? Or
just a coincidence? Could I somehow get into her closet

and have a quick look through those boxes? Of course, I supposed the cops had checked them out already. After what I'd said to Andy, he would have taken care of it himself—if it had not been done before.

I jotted down more questions.

Weather girl? I wrote. *How is she involved?*

Who would want to harm BOTH Allie and her mother? Were their deaths connected?

I looked up from my notebook when I heard the tinkling of the bell that signaled *customer!* An attractive young brunette gave me the kind of smile you'd give an audience of thousands—as opposed to a single bookstore owner frowning at a notebook. This woman loved the spotlight, I decided. But despite the mega-wattage of her smile, my instinct was to like her; the friendliness seemed genuine. And I was good at reading people, just like I was at reading books.

Somehow, she seemed familiar, but I couldn't place her.

"Welcome," I called out. "I'm glad that there are readers who don't let a little rain keep them from their books."

Beside me, Gatsby let out an enthusiastic bark. A stillness always seemed to settle over us on rainy days like this, and Gatsby didn't like it. He liked busyness and people.

Oliver scampered out from behind the self-help shelf to check out the guest as well.

"What an awful weather week!" She put her umbrella in a corner and brushed some rain off of her coat. Still beaming from ear to ear, she jokingly held both hands up, as if to defend herself. "But it's not my fault! Don't blame me for the rain! It's the skies that did it. We should blame the clouds."

Blame *her? For the weather? What an odd remark*, I thought. And that's when it hit me: this was Regina Whatley. As in *the* Regina Whatley: *Watching the Skies For Your Commute, Dependable and Accurate, Covering the Harbor from North to South and East to West on Your Favorite—Channel 8.*

I quickly closed my notebook lest she see that she herself had figured in my musings. Speaking of coincidences...

"Is Elizabeth around?" she asked. "I have a letter for her project."

"No, she's off today. But I can get it to her, and, of course, here is your coupon. Five percent off of any book we carry in the store." I handed her a coupon from the stack underneath the counter. "And thank you for your contribution."

"Oh, that's great," she said. "I don't have much time, but I think I will have a quick peek around the store. Do you have *The Gold Pelican?* I really loved the movie, and I heard it was a book."

"A lovely book," I said. "Let me show you where it is."

On any other day, this would be my cue to grumble to myself. How could so much intrigue wait in a book, unread, until the story made its way to the movie multiplexes? Then it was "discovered!" As if it were something new.

Elizabeth and I had almost choked one day when a teenage boy happened to come across book one of *The Lord of the Rings*. He was almost breathless with excitement. "Hey, man!" he'd called out to his friend, "the movie was so great that someone went and made the film into a book." Then he turned to us. "This must be brand-new. When did this come out?"

Elizabeth had smiled. "The fifties, I believe."

But now I didn't care. I just wanted to lay my eyes on that letter as soon as possible. Might it contain a hint about why my buddy Houston was so anxious to have a word with our local weather expert? How odd would that be if the answer had appeared almost as soon as I had written down the question in my book: *Weather girl? How is she involved?*

Of course, the letter in my hand might just be about some trip or other family news, nothing about the Carringtons or Houston. *Don't get too excited, Rue.*

As I rung up her purchase, I thanked her for the letter.

"I think it's a good one," she said. "It's from my mother to *her* mom, and it lets me see the way her mind worked back when she was young. This was when she first moved here to Massachusetts. My grandmother was in Iowa and was very frugal way back then about her phone bill and all. So my mom wrote lots of letters. And my grandma was a saver. She saved every single one." She glanced at the envelope, which still lay on the counter. "It's great to read something that your mother wrote when she was even younger than you are today. And she pours her heart out here. Oh, you know how it is: when you're in your twenties, you don't mind sharing with the world every single thing you feel. By the time I came along, she was not like that all. So practical! All business. *No TV before your homework* and *All those dirty dishes won't wash themselves, you know.*"

"Yes, I think Elizabeth is onto something good. You can really find some treasures tucked into envelopes."

As anxious as I was to peek into one specific envelope, there was something I knew I should do first for Elizabeth. If fate had not brought Regina in to give me a clue, perhaps she had been brought in for another reason: so that I could make a plea on behalf of the Literacy Foundation of Southeastern Massachusetts.

I floated my idea for a TV piece about the letters project.

"I love that idea!" She flashed that smile again. "Of course, I just do the weather, but I know that my friend Ben will be all over that. You can tell Elizabeth that he'll be calling her real soon." She thought for a moment. "Do you think she'll go on camera?"

"To promote the book, she will. This is her passion project and, of course, she loves the cause."

"Oh, we love that kind of thing as well. It's just the kind of story that viewers want the most. Secrets and family drama as revealed in letters! Money for a good cause, people helping people, all of that good stuff. Well, I have to run. But we will be in touch for sure." She gave me a little wave. "As we like to say at Channel 8, *wishing you sunshine and clear skies!* Although it doesn't look like you'll be getting much of that today."

She turned back to me before she made it to the door. "I do hope she likes my letter. I heard she wanted letters with links to local history. And my mother used to sing at the Eighth Street Café. Do you know the place? She writes about it in the letter."

I could barely get the words out. "Yes. I had some soup there just the other day."

As soon as she was out the door, I peeked in the envelope, which, thankfully, wasn't sealed—although

Elizabeth would not have cared a whit if I'd opened it to look.

Hi Mama! How are you?

How I wish you could see Massachusetts with its blue, blue waters and charming little towns. Although SOME of your wishes have not come true for me, I want you to know that I am happy—SO MUCH happier than I ever dreamed I could be. And I want you to know as well that I intend to keep my promise. If I can't support myself with music after these five years, I WILL go back to school. But, I know somehow, Mama, that my plan will work. I know it is meant to be. Why else would I feel so alive, so much at peace, so true to myself when I am singing?

I've written three new songs that I'd love for you and Dad to hear. And the café's such a special place, kind of like a family full of people who love the things I do. And I don't just mean the music. The owners and the other kids care a lot about the things that are impor-tant to me too. Like the environment. And kindness. They put people before things. Most people really don't. That is a thing I've noticed.

You should meet Corinne and Rob! For them, it's not about the money or the food or how big a crowd comes to see our shows. (Although sometimes there's a nice-sized group waiting to hear us sing!) For them, it's about me and all the others with dreams of making music. What they're all about is giving us a chance!

You should see the place. The Eighth Street Café is the cutest small blue building by the water, and to me, it's magic.

Please come if you can.

Love and miss you always,

Leslie (Budding Superstar!)

Who was Rob? I jotted down the name in my list of things to be investigated.

I also found myself intrigued with the idea of Corinne as described in Leslie's letter. Rather than a black sheep, she sounded like a good soul. Perhaps Elizabeth and Andy had more information they could share about Catherine's twin.

CHAPTER EIGHT

s the rain continued to keep the customers away, I had more time to think. I became more convinced than ever: Allie's murder *had* to be connected to her mother's death, despite what Andy thought. I had to see those boxes! I hated the idea of Allie's killer running free, and the police, as usual, seemed to be determined to chase after the wrong leads.

The cops might have checked the boxes, but I had the feeling they'd failed to look through the contents as closely as they should have. They seemed to be convinced that Allie's mother and her things had no connection to this latest death.

Rue, you're not a cop, Andy told me in my head.

But I was a reader, which meant I knew a lot of things. Like that "coincidences" should never be ignored. They always led you somehow to a satisfying ending that took most people by surprise (if the author knew her craft).

So I made a plan. I grabbed a little gift to take to Barry in a show of sympathy (combined with a little sleuthing). It was a leather notebook with a saying about measuring our days in love rather than in years. Allie had told me once she liked it, so it was a piece of her, plus a place for him to write down things about their time together. Mostly, of course, it was a way to get inside her apartment—and hopefully the closet with the boxes. That would be kind of tricky, but I had to try.

For good measure, I stopped by the sandwich shop and bought some of Melba's good corn chowder along with a shrimp-salad sandwich, also a specialty. I hoped it was something Barry might have chosen and something he would eat; he had to keep up his strength.

Then I continued on my mission with a vague sense of unease lodged inside my chest. Barry didn't even know me, and here I was heading off to Allie's to intrude on the poor man's grief. But if I could figure out this puzzle and identify the person who had killed his fiancée? He'd think that was more than worth the trouble of a stranger barging in; I was sure of that.

Hopefully the boxes had not been hauled off to the station. I realized with a start that's how it would have happened if this was *Law and Order: Special Victims Unit*. Except this was *Somerset Harbor Police: We Don't Have a Clue*. (Except, of course, for Andy. My buddy might be stubborn, but he knew his stuff.)

I dropped the pets at home, happy to see that Andy hadn't gotten there before me. He, of course, would want to know what I was running off to do. And a trip to see the bereaved fiancé would be frowned upon by my nitpicky friend. I'd be "getting too involved."

After making the short drive to Allie's, I knocked on her apartment door with my heart in my throat. I had to admit it. Andy would have had a point if he'd had a chance to scold me. I was intruding on a man who had the right to be left the heck alone. But to my great relief, he looked glad to see me, although a tad surprised.

"Ah," he said. "A friendly face." He glanced down at the takeout I held in my hand. "That smells awfully good, although you really didn't have to."

"When I need a quick meal, I always go to Melba's. It really is the best, and with all that you've been through, well, I just imagined that you might forget to get yourself some dinner."

Ruefully, he shook his head. "You know what? I did! And it's just now hit me that I'm hungry. I think I skipped lunch as well."

I handed him the bag. "Did you know I used to do

this kind of thing for Allie? On inventory day, I'd take that sweet girl a sandwich, and I'd say, 'Allie, eat!'"

He smiled. "She could be forgetful."

"One of her very favorite things was to watch the lighted boats sail by in a parade at the start of summer season. But if I didn't text her to go out to the pier, it would slip the girl's mind. Every single time." I sighed. "I sure will miss our Allie."

"Yeah. My to-list always had the words *Tell Allie to remember to...* do something or the other. But the thing about it was, if something was important to another person, she'd remember that. Like a birthday maybe. I don't think I've ever known a person who had a bigger heart, and I don't think I ever will."

I looked around the room. There was an empty mug that had must've held her final cup of coffee. On the table was her copy of a new mystery novel, opened to a page that she would never read. I had recommended it last week.

"Please. Won't you have a seat?" He sat down at the table and dug into the chowder. "Have half of the sandwich. There's enough for two."

"Oh no, you go ahead. This is all for you." Of course, what I really wanted was to get into that bedroom and the closet. "Is there anything at all that I can help you with here in the apartment?" Then I thought of something. I sat across from him and said to him gently, "If you're not up for doing it, I'd be more than happy to go through Allie's things and find something nice for her to wear—of course, with your approval."

I hesitated and took a cleansing breath. It seemed, well, just wrong to be less than truthful to a grieving man. But I was doing it, I told myself, for the best of reasons. Plus, I knew Allie's tastes. This really was a way that I could be of use.

"But you have to understand that I don't want to intrude. Only if it's something that you feel you're not up for doing," I said to him sincerely.

He looked up from his chowder. "You know, that would be amazing. I'm not any good at picking women's clothes, and I'm sure that you'd know better what she would have wanted." He looked down on the table. "This is just surreal. I can't believe that this is what we're doing. Picking out her clothes for *this?* Those clothes should be for parties. They should be for going out. Who did this, Rue? Who did it?" He looked down at the table and put his head in his hands.

I reached out to touch his elbow. "I can't imagine, Barry."

But I intended to find out.

I hesitated for a moment. "Barry," I began, "did Allie mention anything at all that might have made her nervous or upset in the last week or so? Did she give you any clue who might have done a thing like this?"

"Not that I can think of. I talked to her that night. And she seemed to be just fine. It seemed to me like she was having just a normal week."

Hopefully, he'd stick around in town after the services for Allie. I'd love to ask him more, but for now, I'd let him grieve—while I checked out some things in Allie's room.

The room was just as I'd imagined: clothes and shoes and books strewn across the bed and chair and littering the floor. "Being neat and tidy is for losers," she had told me once. "Such a waste of time." She'd been too busy living life to put away her things. Maybe she had sensed that her life would be short.

Tossed over a chair, I spotted a blue and white wrap dress that I'd once admired on her, causing her to throw her head back and laugh. "Oh Rue, would you believe that I was late to a client meeting because I saw this dress? It was in the window of Beach Sophisticate, and I had to try it on."

In a nutshell, that was Allie: never one to say no to a dress or a dessert or to coffee with a friend. Never mind that the dress would almost certainly be right there for her to buy after she'd finished with her meeting.

I picked it up and studied it. It looked clean, unwrinkled, good to go. I remembered that she'd worn it with a necklace that had a small pink stone. I checked the tangle of gold and silver jewelry on her dresser and—voila!—there it was. Allie could be buried in an outfit she had loved. I felt tears begin to form, but there was no time for that. I had a job to do.

Next: a quick look in the closet. If Barry caught me looking in the boxes, I might have to explain. Or I could say that I was looking for a scarf or some accessory to go with the chosen dress.

Luckily, the boxes were right there by the door once I stepped into the closet. *From Mama's House* was scrawled on strips of masking tape on the tops of both. A quick peek inside revealed that there were letters, photo albums, and newspaper clippings. I also saw a couple of hardbound books of poetry and a few carefully wrapped china figurines.

What would have upset Allie? The yellowed stories from the paper didn't seem to be the answer. They were mostly boring stuff, although there was no time to study every single one. One showed Catherine's father holding up a plaque, surrounded by his family. Catherine and Corrinne seemed to be about eight or nine, and I was startled to discover that they looked just alike: same eyes, same chin, same hair, same delighted smile as if the cameraman were telling them a joke. I'd known that they were twins, but no one had told me that they were identical.

I picked up an envelope near the top of a box. The letter was addressed to *Corinne Wright, 482 Poughkeepsie Way, Albany, New York.* The return address was Catherine's, and there was no postmark; the envelope had never made it into the mail.

I took out the letter.

This is to state that you are to have no further contact with Alexandra Lane, my minor child, your niece. My attorney's in the process of filing a restraining order. But I want to put on paper the hurt and anger that I feel.

You've taken things too far! And I am appalled. Allie is my life. And my child is the one thing in this world that you are not allowed to bring into your feud with Daddy.

I am shocked and saddened to be betrayed like this—and by my own twin sister. When no one else would speak to you, I came to visit you and made sure that we stayed close. And now you use the most precious thing I have to be a pawn in your twisted game.

Do not contact me anymore. This will be our last
communication. We may be kin by blood. My face
may be your face, but our hearts are far more different
than I ever thought they were. If this is how you treat a
sister, I'd much prefer to live my life as an only child.

I felt the kind of chill that Allie must have felt. But what did it mean exactly? What was the awful thing that Corinne had done to Allie?

That's when I noticed there was something else tucked into the envelope. It was another letter, written in another, bolder hand.

I have Allie, Dad. And there's no need to worry. Allie is
just fine! And you and my "Miss Perfect" sister need to
just chill out. There is no need to panic like you always
do. Of course, I'd never hurt her.

But if you and Cathy want her back, I'll need to have
some money, which of course you'll give me—as you
should have long ago.

Isn't it so stupid that it's come to this?

I've never asked for much. It's fine that you disown
me! It's fine that I don't live the garish, showy lifestyle

of a snooty Carrington. All I ask for is a small check to keep my café open, so that young musicians might get half a chance to live the kind of lives they want.

You'd spend it on a car, Dad. You'd spend it on a trip. Why not spend on your daughter? And if you hate me that much, do it for the kids, the kids who want to sing and make music for the world. According to your website, your company is big on "making contributions to the betterment of youth."

Hmm. Could have fooled this girl.

You know my P.O. Box. You can send the money there. Meanwhile, me and Allie are off on an adventure. A zoo might be involved—or plays or a museum. It will all be Allie's choice. I really love this kid and wish I'd had the chance to get to know her better. That's another thing that you took from me (and her).

I stared at the letter. *Unbelievable,* I thought. Corinne had *kidnapped Allie?*

I wondered what had happened next. *Someone* had saved the restaurant. I supposed the money came from Allie's grandfather to get her back. And years after that, it supposedly was Catherine who had bailed her sister out with another gift. Hard to believe, I thought, after her traitor of a sister had gone and pulled a thing like that. So much for *no communication.*

Still shaken up by what I'd read, I could not imagine how Allie must have felt when she'd read those letters. Judging from her shock, she must have been unaware of the dark undertones of her "adventure" with her aunt.

Where was Corinne today? Could she have poisoned Allie and Allie's mom before her?

I put the letters back, shut the closet door, and hung the blue dress on a hanger with the necklace. Then I took the dress to Barry. "Allie loved this dress," I said, "and she looked so pretty in it. What do you think of this one?"

He gave me a sad smile. "I think that one's perfect. I loved her in that dress. Rue, I can't thank you enough."

"Glad to help," I said. "Is there someone I can call? Some of Allie's relatives perhaps?" I paused. "I seem to recall that she had an aunt—Corinne?" *Please tell me more about her,* I begged him in my head.

"Oh yeah. Allie loved her aunt! But she's been dead for years—a car accident, I think. Or so Allie understood. She and Allie weren't in touch."

"Well, that's too bad," I said. "Since Allie lost her mother at an early age, it would have been really nice to have an aunt step in."

He dug his hands into his pockets. "Yeah, that was such a shame." He gave me a rueful smile. "Rich people and their problems, right? Allie never talked about it all that much. It was the one thing in her life, I think, that hurt to her core—all the drama in her family. She loved her Grandpa Peter and would visit him a lot before he died. But she never liked the way that he just disowned Corinne. He just cut his daughter out of the family fortune—out of the family's life. Never spoke to her again! And why? He was supposedly embarrassed by the way she lived her life. She did not live with the *decorum* that he would have liked for her to have, as if that's a reason not to have your daughter in your life."

"What was she like?" I asked.

"Oh, from what I understand, she was free with men. I heard she drank too much, experimented with some drugs. And Peter Carrington? Well, that guy held himself up to be some grand example of strong virtues. One of those very showy, ultraconservative, family-values kind of guys."

"Yeah. Nothing says *family values* like kicking your own daughter out of your family's life."

"I think the final straw was when she got onto a health kick, opened up an all-natural restaurant, and told everyone she knew that—and this is rich—children should eat healthy and stay away from candy except a little at a time. Of course, that didn't suit the CEO of Something Sweet Confections."

"Oh, I can imagine!" I carefully laid the dress across a chair and settled in across from him at the table. "So, Allie never saw her aunt?"

"There were times she did, but it wasn't very much. Allie's mother kept up with Corinne a little when Allie was a kid. They were twins, you know; they had that kind of bond that twins sometimes have. But if they saw each other—or if they even wrote—it had to be a secret. Which was nuts, because Catherine could have lost it all —her whole inheritance—just by talking to her sister." He shook his head, pausing to brush some hair from his eyes. "But this one time, Allie told me, she and her Aunt Corinne got to go off by themselves on a little trip. And Allie said her aunt was crazy—in a good way, not bad. So different from her mother! And Allie loved her mother; she and her mom were tight. But Catherine was the quiet twin, and I guess Corinne was more the type to set off on an adventure."

He paused to take one last bite of sandwich. "I never had the pleasure of meeting Allie's mom. But Allie said that everything with Catherine was done in a certain order. Everything was just so, all planned out, all refined. But Corinne, it seemed, moved as the spirit led her and, to a nine-year-old, the whole thing was just a blast. They traveled around to state parks, and they did some hiking, if I remember right. Allie said she still thought of the songs and stories they made up along the way. At least, she had that memory."

Until she learned the truth about that little trip.

"Sounds amazing," I said.

"One of the best weeks of her life! That's what Allie said. And it really hurt her that she never got to see her aunt again. I guess it all had to do with the family's feud. But why involve a child? Why not let her see her aunt? Later, when she was grown up, Allie made an effort to reach out to Corrine. She lived right here in town—for a while, at least. But I guess that the ugliness had gone too far by then."

CHAPTER NINE

he next day, the rains returned, coming down in sheets with thunder in the distance, to the great chagrin of Gatsby. He'd find the smallest little cubbyholes around the store to try to squeeze himself into whenever there were storms. Now, he was whining pitifully at me from underneath the low shelf that housed our poetry collection. Next to him Oliver was perched, as if the little cat had sensed that he could be of comfort to the sad-eyed dog.

Elizabeth and I were moving about the store, selecting books we loved for a special table I was setting up in front. I'd written out a sign in the calligraphy my grandmother had taught me when I'd visit as a child. *For Your Rainy Days,* I'd written, *Elizabeth and Rue Recommend:*

Rain was in the forecast for the next few days, which meant the store would be fairly empty. But it wouldn't hurt to throw out a few suggestions to those who braved the storms.

I pulled from the shelves a copy of an old classic, adding it to the table as I continued to tell Elizabeth about the letters and the talk I'd had with Barry. "Something doesn't fit," I said. "If Corinne would do a thing like that—take her sister's child—why on Earth would Catherine still lend money to her sister?"

Elizabeth paused to think. "Well, that *was* a long time later. A lot of things could have happened in between."

"Still! Some things you can't forgive. And I would think that what Corinne did with Allie would make it onto that list."

"Oh, yes. Absolutely." Elizabeth paused to think.

I saw a flash of inspiration move across her eyes.

Excellent, I thought. She must have had some insight into the situation with the twins, which was a real good thing. This pseudo-sleuth was stumped.

But instead, she'd thought of a book to add to our table. She dashed across the room. "*News of the World!*" she called out. "Have you read it, Rue? You should."

My mind was still on Allie and the mystery of her death.

"This was the perfect book," said Elizabeth, adding it to the display.

"And the perfect meal today," I said, "would be a bowl of soup. From the Eighth Street Café. Delivered by a waiter or a waitress who's been there long enough to know some history on the place."

When my part-timer Ellen came at noon, Elizabeth and I headed out for lunch.

"Bon appétit!" called Ellen. "I'll give some extra love to Gatsby. I know your boy hates the rain."

Thankfully, the rain had slowed a bit as Elizabeth drove us to the restaurant, whose parking lot seemed packed despite the dismal weather.

"They do a good business at this place," Elizabeth observed.

The hostess seated us at one of the only empty tables and handed us some menus. I was trying to decide—butternut squash soup with goat cheese or split pea and potato—when I noticed that a waitress was standing over us. How long had she been there?

"You guys gonna order?" she asked impatiently. "Or what exactly is the deal?" It was the same young girl who'd waited on me before.

"A *hello* would be nice." Elizabeth looked startled. "And we're doing fairly well. You were so nice to ask," she said sarcastically. She was not afflicted with my need to

PENNY BROOKE

be overly polite even in the face of rudeness. "We'll start with the muffin basket while we look the menu over."

"I'll take some apple tea," I said.

Elizabeth settled back against the seat. "And I'd like a coffee."

The girl was off without a word.

"With a little cream," Elizabeth called out to the back of the retreating waitress. Then she turned to me and mumbled, "A little manners. Please! Have you ever in your life?" She picked up her menu. "I don't know if I'm more upset by that young woman's rudeness or by the fact that I sound like my third-grade teacher, who I used to think was far too old to even be alive."

After twenty minutes, we still didn't have our drinks and had yet to order. My stomach was now grumbling in protest. Looking over menus always made me hungry.

I looked around and saw the girl standing in a corner, staring intently at her phone. Then she glanced toward the door and smiled. A small group of teens had entered, including a tall boy who she held steadily in her gaze. She tossed her hair and smiled. Then she went back to her phone, pretending not to watch him.

"Well, we've really lost her now," said Elizabeth.

So much for a chatty waitress full of information

about the history of the place. At the moment I would have settled for a very quiet waitress who would *just bring me some food.*

I flagged down an older man as he delivered a muffin basket to the table next to ours. "Excuse me, please. Hello!" I called. "Our waitress seems to have become... distracted." I glanced over at another table, where she was holding a muffin to the tall boy's mouth. "I was hoping you could take our orders or find someone who can."

He followed my gaze to the waitress, who had now taken a seat at the table with the other kids. A look of dismay crossed his eyes. "Oh, ma'am, I'm *so* sorry." He pulled out his notebook. "Do you know what you would like?"

After we had given him our orders, he told us that the food would be right out with desserts on the house. Then he lowered his voice to a confidential tone. "That's the owner's daughter, or else she'd be long gone. We've all tried to tell Rob that he needs to be more forceful with Adriana there. But, well, he's the boss, so what can you really do?"

Rob. Why did that name sound familiar? Then I thought about the letter Regina Whatley had brought in for Elizabeth's book project. *You should meet Corinne and*

Rob. So Corinne's former partner was still here at the café.

"Her attitude is not at all in keeping with the spirit of the business." The waiter was being very careful to speak in such a way that he would not be overheard. I noticed that his nametag said his name was Jim. "But I guess she needs the work to put more gas in the Lexus that her daddy bought her," he continued with a frown. "Plus, that girl is crazy for some jewelry and some shoes —and most of those are also bought by Daddy, I suppose. I know for sure they don't come from what she's making here. I've seen the prices on those shoes— and I've also seen the numbers on our checks," he added with another frown.

"Looks like the place is making money," I said as I looked around. Then I exchanged glances with Elizabeth. She must have been thinking the same thing: this Jim sure talked a lot for a man with tables to look out for—not to mention picking up the slack for Adriana. But if it would help me in my quest for truth, I would happily wait a little longer for my soup (with apologies to my growling stomach).

"Business has been awesome—better than it's ever been," our waiter said. "And I've been around a while. But lately, I have to say that the vibe here has been weird. Rob has really been on edge, especially since that guy in the corner showed back up in town. He used to work here once, and if I had to guess, he has some beef with Rob. But whatever's going on, that guy right there is real bad news. He's upsetting Rob, and when the boss isn't happy, that's no good for anyone."

I glanced over to see none other than Roger Houston sporting his trademark scowl. He appeared to be engaged in a fierce argument with a woman across the table from him. Then I recognized her; it was Regina Whatley. Her eyes were opened wide, and she looked alarmed. Her arms and hands were flying through the air as she tried to make a point.

Then I noticed Roger bark some kind of order directed at Adriana, who got up lazily from the table and returned with a cup of coffee, which she delivered with a roll of her eye.

"Well, let me put your order in." Jim at last began to move off from our table. "And then I suppose I should check on her other customers before somebody starves."

The food soon came as promised, and we wolfed our meals down quickly, as hungry as we were. With my stomach finally full, I could think more clearly, and I distilled my mission into a single goal: I wanted Jim to tell me how this place was linked to Allie.

And so when he returned with our complimentary chocolate-chip banana bread, I had a question for him.

In a trick I'd learned from Andy, I put the question to him without seeming to have asked him anything at all. "You know, the two of us had planned to come in this week with our dear friend Allie, who has since passed away. I guess you might have heard. It was big news here in town."

"Allie Lane? Oh, yes! She's been in here quite a bit— just in the last few weeks. But I noticed that this last time, she and Rob, the owner, seemed to be having a...*discussion,* shall we say. And neither one looked pleased. Your friend looked real upset. Oh, and let me say, so sorry for your loss. Seemed like a real nice girl. Awful thing that happened. I hope they catch the creep."

Allie arguing with Rob? *Getting closer,* I thought. If this was a game of Clue, I might guess the following: Someone from the café—in Allie's bedroom—with a dose of poison. But there were important questions left: like exactly who and why.

My thoughts were interrupted by an outcry from the corner. I swiveled to catch a glimpse of Regina standing up, yelling frantically for help.

What was happening?

A glance down answered my question.

Below her, sprawled out on the floor, was Roger Houston.

And chaos quickly followed.

Once the medical attendants and police had come and gone, Somerset Harbor had been left with its second sudden and suspicious death in just a few days' time.

Once the coroner had announced his findings, the people of our quiet town were left shocked and afraid about who might be next.

Like Allie had before him, Roger Houston had been poisoned.

he next few days were a blur. As rumors flew after the latest murder, we gathered to mourn Allie at the small St. Leo's Church at the edge of town. Everyone, it seemed, had an angle or a theory about what might have really happened on the night that Houston died. Over lattes, lobster rolls, or evening cocktails by the pier, we asked each other questions that no one could really answer: why was Houston here, and how was this surly being connected to our Allie?

Allie's services were packed with friends and a few reporters from across the state and beyond. The esteemed Carringtons had always been newsworthy. Now, you had the added twist of a likely murder (seem-ingly connected to another). Elizabeth had forwarded a story that she'd seen on the website of a paper all the way in Vermont. *Chocolate Heiress Murdered? Details Not So Sweet as Second Victim is Discovered Poisoned.*

As the crowd filed out, I noticed a few plainclothes cops standing toward the back. They were watching carefully while appearing nonchalant. I knew what they were up to: killers very often liked to insert themselves among the mourners at services and vigils. (I'd been known to pump Andy for the details of his often-sordid work. As a book person through and through, I was all about the details of other people's lives.)

Speaking of my cop friend, he was being frustratingly tight-lipped—even worse than usual. And, of course, he was super busy.

Now he sat beside me at the church as we stared down at Allie's face on the program for the services. "She was something special, right?" Andy asked me with a sigh. "I wish we could have sent her off with the monster put away for good, just like he deserves."

By that time, all of the mourners had moved out of the church, but I hated to get up, as if some last bit of Allie might still linger in the church. That was the mature me. The other part of me longed to hear from Andy five little magic words: *Yes, Rue, you were right.* I was still convinced that Allie's murder had its roots in things that had begun long before the day Roger Houston came to town.

I turned toward him in my seat. "Now, don't you agree that the monster who killed Allie wasn't Houston after all?" I talked in a low voice, although most everyone had gone. "It couldn't have been him, Andy. Unless there are *two* killers here in town with poison as their *modus operandi*."

"Well, it's more complicated than we thought. I can say that without a doubt." He sighed and glanced down at his watch. "And there's another meeting at the station in a little bit—to make me miss my nap. You just wait till you get older! You *look forward* to a nap. You *anticipate* a nap. I never thought I'd see the day. But with all that's going on, it's all-hands-on-deck, which I can understand. And now with the press all on this, it's like a whole new fire has been lit under the chief."

"You're the best they've got. They really need you, Andy."

"I'm supposed to be retired, you know. Except for a few well-chosen cases—for private clients, mostly."

"And Allie's is a case you know you would have picked. Even if the chief hadn't come and pulled you in."

"Oh, yeah. You know that I won't stop until there's justice for our girl—well, the closest thing to justice that is ours to give. But the second victim in this thing is not the kind of guy I'd ever choose to get off my couch to help."

"Except for the fact that if we find out who murdered—"

He gave me that look that was reserved for only me.

I made the correction quickly. "What I mean is that if *you* find out who murdered Houston, that will help us— umm, *you*—solve Allie's murder too."

He stood up to stretch. "That is the very reason that I'm all in on this one."

I looked him the eye. "Tell me, Andy, please. Now that we are fairly certain that he's not the person who hurt Allie, can you tell me now? What was it about Houston that made you zero in on him?"

Andy hesitated. "Well, it's still an open case. The old rules still apply. Confidentiality is still a vital thing."

"Oh, come on. Just spill it. Just tell me that one thing."

Andy shook his head and smiled. "Girl, you make me tired. You make me want to tell you just so I can get some rest from question after question."

Feeling very hopeful, I settled back into my seat.

Silence filled the room.

Patiently, I gave him my best smile. "I'm waiting. Please continue."

He laughed and shook his head. "Now, you understand that this is not to be repeated. And this is all you get. It's all I'm gonna say, okay?"

I nodded.

Andy paused. "The guy was seen with Allie the day before she died, and whatever he was saying, it had our girl in tears."

"He upset a lot of people from what I understand. Like Rob from the café."

"Yeah, that's what we're hearing, Rue. Apparently, he worked there—quite a few years ago, from what I understand. Some were so glad to see him back and some of them not so much. But all that they will tell us is that he was unpleasant and demanding of the waiters. He didn't like the way the place was being run. He didn't like the changes to the menu, the lack of upkeep on the place…"

"But why would he even care if he was just a guy who used to work there?"

"I think that question's key. When we talked to Rob, the owner, he claims the guy was just a pest. But, of course, there has to be a whole lot more to it than that."

"So Rob is holding out?"

"That seems to be the case."

I thought about that for a moment. "What's the deal with Houston's background? Where did the guy come from? And what exactly does he do? Or *did* he do, I guess."

Andy raised an eyebrow. "You and your questions, Rue." He sighed. "I guess it can't hurt to tell you that the guy was in insurance. He was born in Boston, spent some time here in the Harbor, and settled in New Hampshire after that. Divorced, two kids, one dog."

"Hmm. Might not have been as much of a jerk as we first supposed. Perhaps his crusty nature covered up a softer side. Perhaps he was complex!"

"This is a murder, Rue, not some dramatic novel that you're selling at the bookshop." Then he thought about it. "Okay, Rue, what gives? Out of curiosity—and that is all it is—what about his bio reveals a *softer side?*"

"Well, the dog of course!"

He rolled his eyes. "Of course. Care to get some lunch? Then I'm heading to the station. In addition to the meeting, we're hoping we can talk one more time to Barry Lyman before he gets out of town. But I don't think that's gonna happen—he's got some stuff for work he has to hurry back to. I guess that's the way it goes for a young man on the rise."

"Well, I suppose that's good, you know? He might welcome the distraction."

There was a private burial that I supposed was going on right now. Barry, I imagined, would head home after that. I studied the elaborate pattern on the carpet as I thought of the life he could have had with Allie. "Allie found a good one," I mused out loud to Andy.

"The guy's just all torn up," he said. "But I don't know. I wonder…"

"You wonder? About Barry?"

"Something doesn't fit." Then he caught himself. "Oh Rue, there you go. You know as well as I do—I can't talk about the case!"

As I watched the light play against the stained glass windows, I pondered Allie's fiancé, who had seemed almost perfect. What had Andy noticed?

He had seemed to be devoted—and understandably distraught; there was nothing in his grieving process that would raise any questions. Plus, I knew that Allie, despite her scattered ways, was wise beyond her years when it came to the people she let get close to her. Despite the miles between them, Barry seemed to have been attentive. In fact, he'd talked to Allie the very night she died.

I thought back to our conversation. *I talked to her that night. And she seemed to be just fine. It seemed to me like she was having just a normal week.*

But now that I thought about it, she hadn't been *just fine.* She had just discovered that a "fun" trip with a late aunt had a much darker side. She'd found out that her mother had been keeping secrets. And, as if that was not enough, this Roger Houston had appeared—for whatever reason—and caused her great distress. If she and

Barry were that close, it seemed very odd she would not confide in him.

Had her relationship with Barry not been what it seemed? In the last year or so, I had been a little jealous of the warmth that always filled her eyes when she'd talk about him.

Don't let it be him, I thought. *Please let it be Rob. Or a disgruntled worker who was fired from Something Sweet. Anyone but him.*

"Oh, I'm sure that Barry's fine," I said to Andy. "Unless there's something that you..." I let my voice trail off. But Andy wasn't biting; he knew my games by now.

With both of us having to get back, we stopped for a quick bite at The Blue Crab, where I had a healthy salad and stole fries from Andy's plate. We had managed to snag an outdoor table to enjoy the sun, which had finally decided to shine down on our rain-soaked town.

I was spearing a tomato when I heard raised voices to my left. At a table just a little ways away, a young girl was leaning forward toward an older man, speaking intently to him. I recognized that whine! It was Adriana, our neglectful waitress. Her tears had left dark streams of mascara running down her cheeks.

Andy saw where I was looking.

"Is that Rob from the café?" I asked, thinking that the older man had to be her father.

"That would be him." He nodded.

"With his daughter, Adriana." I stole another fry.

"You don't say." He watched them closely. "I'd say something's up."

The father pointed at his daughter in an emphatic gesture. I could see a fury boiling in him just below the surface.

The girl appeared to be in the midst of some tirade. I couldn't understand her words, but her strident tone caused some of the nearby diners to turn around and stare.

I took a sip of water. "She's a waitress at his place." I made a face. "And not a very good one."

"I wish that we could hear them." Andy strained to listen as he picked up his coffee cup. Then our view was marred as the couple at the table next to them got up to leave. A busboy cleared it quickly as there was a knot of people waiting to be seated.

I reached for my sweater as I beckoned to our waitress.

"I have a small request," I told her as she hurried to our table. "I seem to have a chill, and I see that table over there is getting lots of sun. Would it be too much trouble if we were to move?"

"Not at all." She smiled.

"Oh, Rue, I'm almost finished, and I really have to

run," Andy interjected. "I was just about to ask her for our check."

"Well, you go on if you have to, but as for me, I would really love to finish up this salad."

Both Andy and the waitress glanced down toward my bowl, which by then was only filled with two small bites of lettuce and a carrot.

The waitress looked from me to Andy in confusion. Should she move our things or not?

"Oh, and dessert, of course," I said. "I always mainly come here for the lovely key lime pie."

Andy smiled at her, and I could see a weariness settle into his eyes. "Yes, I suppose if you could move us, that might be for the best."

As she moved to the new table with our plates, we gathered up our things.

"What on Earth?" asked Andy, speaking quietly. "You're always hot, not cold. And you hate anything that's lime."

"Yes, you're right. I do! I just saw some man who was eating key lime pie, and I had to think real fast."

"What's up with changing tables? I don't get it, Rue."

"Andy, really? No?" I sighed. "Think about it for a moment. You're the smartest cop we have." I spoke in a slow voice, as if I were talking to a child. "Why would you and I prefer to sit at that table over there?" I cut my eyes across the room, where the argument continued between the father and daughter.

I watched his face turn red as comprehension dawned. "Ah, man, I get it now. Rue, I'm so embarrassed. It's a lack of sleep. I have *not* been sleeping well."

As we settled in next to the feuding pair, he gave me a silent nod. "Good job. Thank you, Rue."

In silence, he finished his fish sandwich while we listened to the argument beside us. By that time, they'd decided they should keep their voices down.

We didn't hear whole sentences, but we heard scattered words.

"I can breathe better now for sure," I heard the father say. "But still, I'm thinking that . . ."

"Even at half price, it costs a whole lot more than two hundred lousy dollars," whined the girl. "Two hundred dollars is just nothing."

"Must be very careful . . . not the only one . . . but maybe."

"And the party at Cape Cod . . . those shoes I really wanted . . ."

"With all the . . . and the . . . things *still* are not the same . . ."

"So suddenly I'm dressing like the Little Match Girl? Suddenly we're broke?"

It was kind of odd, like two different conversations:

one about expensive baubles and one about…well, I was not so sure. Perhaps a murder? Maybe?

Suddenly, Adriana stood. "I'm going to Sixth Avenue. Catch you later, Dad."

Andy, Rob, and I looked on as she flounced out of the restaurant and down the sidewalk out of sight.

I bit down on a fry. Sixth Avenue was *not* the place for Little-Match-Girl fashions. I supposed the girl was new at seeking out the sale racks at McCray's on Third and Main.

Her dad paid and left.

"What was that all about?" I said to Andy as the waitress brought my pie.

Andy looked intrigued. "Apparently, this Rob is in financial straits—which I guess might mean the café is in big trouble too. And I suppose that all of this is tied up with the trouble that was brewing between Houston and the restaurant." He paused to think. "Of course, none of the employees mentioned any trouble of a financial nature. So this opens up a whole new line of questions I'd love to explore."

"Financial trouble. That's surprising. Every time I go there, they seem to have a nice-sized crowd."

"You just never know. The food industry is tough. Although, I'm surprised as well." He removed his napkin from his lap and laid it on the table. "Well, this has been enlightening, but I really need to run."

I shoved over my dessert. "First, please eat your pie."

"I didn't order pie. My doctor says no pie!"

"But I can't eat it, Andy. Oh my gosh, it's lime."

He grabbed his fork. "If you insist. There are worse things I have done in the line of investigative duties. For the sake of our town's safety, I will now eat pie."

By the time that he was finished, I knew I really needed to get back to the store. But perhaps Elizabeth might hold down the fort for just a little longer... because I had an idea.

CHAPTER ELEVEN

*A*fter I'd said goodbye to Andy, I punched Elizabeth's number in my cell.

She answered right away. "Hey! How were the services?"

"They did an awesome job. They did right by Allie and, as you might imagine, the place was really packed. How are things going there?"

"Not too bad," she answered. "I've gotten three more letters, and someone came in just now and bought the Narnia collection. You know, that set we carry—the pretty ones in hardback."

"My favorites!" I was pleased.

"She asked me if I thought her grandchildren were too old. I told her that I last read the books myself when I was thirty-two. I was not too old that year, I said to

Mrs. Crocker, and I don't suppose I'll be too old anytime real soon."

"Good job." I gave her a high-five, although, of course, she couldn't see it. "I was thinking that I might run some errands while I'm out," I said. (On Sixth Avenue in particular.) "But if you're starving, I'll come back."

"Oh no, Rue. You go on. Things aren't too busy now, and Alton from the diner brought me a meatloaf plate. He knows I'm like a kid at Christmas when Phyliss makes her meatloaf. And do you know, I think I got an extra helping."

I smiled to myself. "I am thinking Alton might have a little crush!" The owner of the diner was the kindest man I knew and had the bluest, most expressive eyes. He was always coming in for books that I knew he wouldn't read. He'd grab the closest paperback to take to the counter if Elizabeth was working. He'd bought books on losing weight; he was thin as a rail. He'd bought a book on caring for your Golden Doodle—although he owned a Chihuahua.

"Well, he did wave me away when I tried to pay," she said. "We'll see where it goes."

I think she liked him too. Neither one of them was shy—except when they were with each other, which was cute.

I headed to Sixth Avenue, the well-manicured and exquisitely appointed site of the finest shops in town. To be honest, I was thrilled to have an excuse to browse. I didn't come here much. It was way too tempting for a fashion-loving girl. But on the rare occasion, I'd allow myself to visit for a little treat. Just the year before, a white cashmere faux-fur wrap had set me back more than eight hundred dollars when it went on sale as the weather started turning warm. Sometimes I looked at it in my closet, and I cringed when I thought about the price. And sometimes on a cold night, I wrapped myself in its softness just to binge on movies; it felt that luxurious against my skin.

Now, standing at a corner with shops all around me, I tried to figure out which stores might best appeal to a spoiled and whiney teen.

A knot of young girls passed me, all staring at their phones. Perfect, I decided. They were about the same age as the subject I was in pursuit of. I decided that I'd follow, hoping that the girls were in the mood to do a little shopping. Or *more* shopping, I should say. I noticed most of them had bags emblazoned with the names of designers I could neither afford nor pronounce.

Soon enough, they sauntered into a well-lit shop that seemed to carry mostly t-shirts, jewelry, and jeans that were ripped all down the front. I followed them inside, feeling out of place among the youthful clientele. The saleswoman smiled at me in welcome, assuming, I imagined, I was shopping for my daughter. The young girls roamed the aisles, still barely glancing up from the cellphones in their hands.

Next, I followed my little posse into another shop, where something finally managed to wrestle their attention from their tiny screens. A display of boots caused them to shriek so loudly that I almost jumped. As my heart rate returned to normal, they descended on the shoe department while I had a look around the store.

I was fingering a necklace with the most exquisite, delicate ruby charm when I noticed Adriana had joined the group of girls. *Score.* She was telling them a story while they gathered round, some of them with their mouths opened wide in shock. Others clasped their hands over their mouths while they looked at her with wide eyes. In their eyes I saw the drama only teenage girls could feel.

Very nonchalantly, I walked over to the shoes and selected a pair of navy flats with neat bows in blue and gold. Heels just didn't do for long days in the store. I found my size and took a seat with the big gold box, keeping my ears open.

I hoped Adriana wouldn't recognize that I had also been beside her at The Blue Crab that day. Hopefully, in her mind, I was too "way old" to notice. I had certainly been almost invisible that day when she was supposed to be my waitress at the Eighth Avenue Café.

With her story finished, her friends all stood and stared. Then after a stunned silence, they all spoke at once.

"No way!"

"Are you serious?"

"How absolutely tragic."

"I would have cried all day."

"How will you go on?"

"Can I give you a hug?"

Then they descended on her, and more squeals ensued.

If I had not known Adriana, I would have easily assumed they were mourning someone's death. But I was not surprised when she spelled out for them the cause of her deep grief. Her credit card, it seemed, had become maxed out. And now Daddy was no longer willing to pay up and put more room on the card for all the fancy treasures that she craved.

I slipped on the shoes, noting that expensive shoes really *did* feel different from the normal brands I bought. I walked from one end of the shoe department to the next. These shoes were amazing! They were almost like a cushion pressed up against my feet. I had to have these shoes.

"I don't understand," a dark-haired girl said to Adriana. "I thought your father's café was doing really great. Plus, the family money…"

"Well, the restaurant was fine before you-know-who swept in. You know, that awful man I told you about last week. What a total jerk. And then he and my father had this all-out fight. They were screaming at each other. It was bad! Now for some stupid reason, we have to *save our money and spend smart.* How really lame is that?"

No mention of the murder of the man in question. I guess that was second in importance to her lack of spending power.

"What was the fight about?" A tall blonde looked up from her phone to ask the question.

"Who knows? But it's like he made some threat. And all of a sudden now, my dad says that things have got to change back to the way they used to be like a million years ago."

"Like with candlelight and cooking in the fireplace? Like, you know, *pioneers*?"

Adriana scowled. "Are you some kind of fool? No! Like when my dad was young. They used to let these kids come into the place and sing. And then when people came to hear them, they'd sit down at a table and

—here's where it gets weird—it was not required *that they order any food.* So I said to my daddy, how would you make money? And he said they made a little but they never made a lot."

She went on to explain that her dad planned to bring back the program in which aspiring singers could perform on weekend nights. They would be expected to help out in the restaurant. "And this is, like, the absolutely worst plan in the world! They'd get their meals for free! I'll never get to buy a decent pair of jeans again!"

"But how come? I don't get it. Why would they get to eat free and take up all the tables for their singing?" One of the other girls sat down on a bench and ran her finger down a leather boot.

"Because of stupid reasons! Because they're young and want to sing! And now this is their chance. That's what the mean man said."

She said her dad had done the calculations of how much money they might lose and said they had to cut back. "I told him that this guy—that this stranger, really —was not the boss of him. But then he got all funny, and he wouldn't talk about it. *Who is this loser guy?* I said. But my father only said, *It's best we make him happy, Adriana, or he could cause some trouble.*"

What to make of that? Houston had only been a *worker* at the Eighth Avenue Café. He hadn't run the place or owned it. What did he have on Rob that had made the café owner jump through so many hoops to stay in Houston's favor? And now Rob was *still* on edge —even though his nemesis could no longer interfere.

Had it been Rob who'd slipped the poison into something Houston ate or drank? He'd clearly had a motive. And, of course, he had the means since the last meal the victim ate had been served at the café.

But it was clear that Rob was also scared of someone else with some information that could hurt him. I thought back to what I'd overheard that afternoon at lunch. *Must be very careful . . . not the only one.*

I needed to learn more about this Roger Houston and what he might have known. I wondered if Elizabeth had things in her collection about the Eighth Avenue Café in its early days.

How I'd love to talk to Houston! But of course I couldn't. Things had taken quite a turn. He had gone from suspect to the person with the info that could help solve Allie's murder. But by the time I understood that he might be on our side, he was way past telling any of us what he knew.

I reluctantly slipped out of the shiny flats and put my plain brown loafers back on. But I had decided: the spectacular creations in gorgeous midnight blue would be coming home with *moi*. I deserved a treat.

Adriana was now standing by a mirror, holding up a white dress against her body as she slowly turned from side to side.

Her friends all crowded round her.

"You should get it."

"It's so you."

"She can't get it. Don't you *listen*? Because of that stuff with *her card*."

"It is *totally* maxed out? Or like *maybe-kind of* full? With room for one more dress?"

"How can a card be full? Mine always, like, just…works."

Adriana shook her head. "It's totally, like, dead. No good. Nothing. *Nada.* I'm only here to look."

I carefully wrapped the shoes back up in their tissue and snuck a peek at the price.

My heart caught in my throat.

A saleswoman was beside me with her arms outstretched. "I think those are lovely. Can I ring them up for you?"

When I could finally breathe, I gave her my best smile. "I don't think so today. I'm only here to look."

CHAPTER TWELVE

*M*y route back to the store took me past the road that led to the cemetery. On a whim, I decided to drive the short distance to Eternal Garden Estates, where I was sure the burial must have been completed. Perhaps I could catch a glimpse of fresh flowers on the grave.

I wondered who had been there at the private service since Allie had no family left. But I imagined that her Barry, likeable as he was, had friends and family to be with him as they laid his fiancée to rest.

Just across from the cemetery was a small park with a little bar and restaurant right outside the entrance. I noticed several people sitting over drinks at an outside table. One of them was Barry—who I'd thought was in a hurry. What had Andy told me? Something to do with work that Barry had this evening? Should he not have left by now?

But I wouldn't judge the guy. Who wouldn't need a drink with friends after you'd just buried the woman that you planned to marry?

Still, something nagged at me. If he, in fact, had time to stick around in town, why not stop off at the station to answer some more questions as the cops had asked? I knew if it was me, I'd do everything I could to make sure they found the monster and got him locked away.

I drove to a spot where I could turn around and head the other way toward the bookshop. Passing the bar again, I got stopped at a light and had time to look more closely at the small group of mourners. Barry and a woman had moved off to the side. They were arguing, it seemed.

Then I looked more closely. It was the weather girl! What was she doing there? Had she been close enough to Allie that she had been included in the little group of the nearest and the dearest to the recently deceased? I really didn't think so. I'd known Allie fairly well, and she'd never said a word about Regina Whatley.

I thought of the letter that Regina had brought in for the book. It was possible her *mother* might have known Allie's *aunt*. But that did not explain her presence here with Barry and the group. *Very, very strange.*

I was jolted out of my deep thoughts by another driver inching up behind me and laying on the horn.

"Sorry! Going now," I mumbled, and I was on my way.

When I made it to the store at last, Elizabeth was waiting with a cup of tea. "I saw your car pull up, and so I got this started. It's the new ginger peach, which I think is just divine." She handed it to me with a sympathetic look. "I know today was hard."

"So hard. And confusing."

Gatsby came in from the back to happily bark hello and present himself for head rubs.

Since there were no customers at the moment, we settled into the Book Nook to catch up. Where to start exactly? I told Elizabeth about the conversation we had overheard at lunch. I followed with my shopping trip and the things that Adriana had reported to her friends.

I took a sip of tea and petted Oliver, who was nestled, sleeping, on my lap. "So the question is, why was Rob so ready to just jump at the demands of this old employee who breezes into town?"

"And why is he still jumping now that Roger's dead?" Elizabeth looked perplexed. "I think even Philip Marlowe would say this was a stumper." She had always been a big fan of the Raymond Chandler series and its whiskey-loving private eye.

"Did you ever go there, to the Eighth Street Café, in the days when Corinne helped run the place and Houston might have been around?"

Elizabeth was quiet. "No, I don't remember him at all. But I was pretty young back in the heyday of the music and Corrinne. It was a crowded place in those days. *So* much going on." She paused to think some more. "But, hey, do you know what? I might have some stuff back there in the scrapbooks and antiquities. I'll have to check and see." She always tried to maintain some kind of order based on a combination of dates and subject matter. But things were always getting out of order as customers perused her stuff, and a lot of the ephemera fit too many subjects to be pigeonholed into a single category.

I smiled. "I was hoping you would look. Maybe something that you have will give us at least a clue to what the heck is going on."

She nodded knowingly as she sipped her tea. "Sometimes in the past lie all the answers to the present."

"That's really nice. I love it. Who was it who said that?"

"A little bit of wisdom from me, myself, and I."

"Well, of course I know that, but I mean, who said it first?"

"As far as I know, I am."

"Oh. Well then, aren't you the wise one, friend? You should really write that down. Make it into a sign to go above your space."

"Nice idea." She nodded.

A silence fell across the store and we reveled in the quiet, both of us feeling tired.

"Quite an afternoon you've had," Elizabeth said at last, breaking up the silence.

"And that was only part of the weirdness of the day." I leaned against the cushion and closed my eyes to give them a rest. I described the scene at the bar across from the cemetery. "Do you think it's possible that something's up with Barry? Surely not," I said.

"Well, speaking of that subject, here's something else that's weird." Elizabeth leaned forward to look me in the eye. "I can't believe I didn't tell you. The whole thing just slipped my mind, what with all that's happened. I was just about to tell you, and then I got distracted because...well, because of Roger Houston dropping dead right there across from us, right there in the room."

"Understandable," I said. "What is it you forgot?" I wasn't really sure I could take any more excitement, although the day was fairly young.

"That night at the café—the night that Houston died —I saw this guy hanging out in the back of the place.

Not sitting down or eating. He was just kind of watching, looking out of place—and looking mad."

"Do you know who it was?"

"It was Barry! It was him. I'd never met the guy, but I heard someone whisper that he was Allie's fiancé. Because, of course, the whole town was just *fixated* on her story then—and they still are, I guess. I was about to tell you. And then we heard Regina scream."

I paused to take that in. Barry! He had been there at the moment Houston died. "I don't know what to think," I said. "I feel like I'm collecting lots of pieces to the weirdest puzzle ever. But they don't seem to fit together in a way that makes any sense at all."

Elizabeth stood up. "Well, let me head back to my space and see what I might have that's connected to the days of music in the blue house by the bay."

As she headed back, I heard the tinkling of the bell. I looked toward the door, my professional, friendly smile already forming on my face.

"Well, hello there. How are you?" A heavyset young girl gave me an enthusiastic greeting. I pegged her for romances—or biographies perhaps.

"I am lovely. How are you? And welcome." I stood up from my seat.

Gatsby welcomed her as well with his usual enthusiastic bark.

The girl gasped, and a soft look filled her warm, blue eyes. "Oh, I just love Goldens. What is this boy's name? Or perhaps it is a girl."

I smiled. "This is the Great Gatsby, and, as you can tell, he's very pleased to meet you."

"How perfect for a bookstore dog. Do you mind if I pet him?"

"He would absolutely love it. He just adores attention." While she and my dog went about the business of becoming instant besties, I asked what had brought her in. "Can I help you find a book? Or just feel free to browse. We're always getting new stuff in, so it's a great place to explore."

"Just what I love to do. You'll probably have to send me out with a giant box to carry all my books."

From her lips to God's ears. With the awful weather, things had been a little slow.

"My favorite kind of customer," I said.

"But first I have a letter—for Elizabeth?" She fished around a little in her pink leather bag.

"Oh, yes! She's in the back. I can take it for her—unless you'd like to say hello."

She pulled out an envelope. "Either way is fine. It's for her book, of course. With all this awful stuff that's been in the news, I thought about my mother, who was quite the writer, if I do say so myself. Quite the way with words! And this was in a journal that she left me when she died. It's kind of like a letter, so I think that it will count. She left a stack of journals—but not the kind of journal that's filled with private thoughts. They were always meant for me. Because every entry started with *Dear Marianne.* Marianne—that's me."

"Well, isn't that so special?" I took the letter from her as my heart was pounding at the implied connection with the recent tragedies. "I take it she's deceased? If that is correct, I'm sorry."

"Yes, we lost my mother when I was fairly young. I was only seventeen." She began undoing the top buttons of her jacket. "Since she was never very healthy, I think the journal was her way of putting down her thoughts for me to read when I was older. In case I couldn't run to her when I had some crisis because…she might be gone."

"And you were seventeen?" I sighed. "I imagine that was just unbearable for you. We always need our mothers. But what a special woman to do a thing like that. What a thoughtful mother you were blessed with." I looked down at the letter. "And did I hear you mention a connection with the recent news in town?"

"Oh, yes, with that poor Roger Houston and the Eighth Avenue Café. My mother used to sing there, and she had quite the voice—which I did *not* inherit." She stroked the top of Gatsby's head. "Do you know that commercial about Buster's Best Pet Treats? That's my mother's voice that you hear on the TV! Plus she wrote the song. I always thought it was so pretty. Although I have to say, our cats were not big fans of the stuff it advertised."

"I always loved that song. With that soaring melody and all, it always makes me think of romance and adventure and not of little sweeties that I can feed my cat." We shared a laugh at that.

"It's been on the air forever. I feel like it's been so long since she recorded that." She smiled. "It was not her dream, of course, to write songs for commercials. But she had a life in music, and she always said that she got to live her dream because they believed in her at that little blue café. I think Corinne, who ran the thing back then, was kind of like a mother to the kids. Encouraged them and all." She sighed. "It's just a shame they stopped the music there after that lady left. My mother hated that."

"And she knew Roger Houston?"

"Oh, I think that Roger Houston was my mother's one great love. Of course, I would never say that to my father, and they had the nicest marriage—just devoted to each other. But when she talked about this Roger, there was something in her eyes. And somehow, I just knew."

Really? *Roger Houston?* May God rest that man's soul, but I did not believe I'd ever met a less romantic figure.

"Interesting," I said. "I've heard from other people that he was rather...brusque."

"I have heard the same. I think he must have really changed. Back when they were young, those kids from the café were all artistic and *intense.* My mother told me stories. She kept up with some, and all of them were different when they became adults. She always said that was because the world you dream of in your twenties is not the world you get. But Roger took it harder than the rest of them when the music program shut down—and most of the kids, like him, went back to normal, boring lives."

"Was he a singer too?"

"No, he just hung around to support my mother. But they didn't stay together. After a few years, she went on to New York to try to make it there. He stayed on at the café for just a little bit after she was gone. He was kind of a big brother to the kids who came to sing. It was like a family back in those days from what I understand. But then there was some scandal, and Corinne just up and left. And the other guy—her partner—decided he could make a lot more money by just concentrating on the food and drinks. The singers were all out. And like they say in the song, I guess that was the day that the music died."

"What kind of scandal?" I asked.

"She didn't like to talk about it. I could tell it made her sad. She only said there was one. But she didn't say a lot."

I looked down at the letter. "I'd love to have a look—if you don't mind."

"Oh, yes, please! Go ahead. I'd love for you to see it." She was quiet for a moment. "It's kind of magical, that letter. It's my favorite one she wrote. But there is one section in it that I think we shouldn't print. You'll know when you see it. Do you think that's an option? To use just part of it?"

"I will ask Elizabeth. But I don't see why not."

"Great! And maybe I could browse in the non-fiction while you're reading."

"We've got some great non-fiction. In the back and to the left. Happy treasure hunting! And don't forget you'll get a coupon since you brought in a letter. Five percent off of any book."

With that, she was off. Gatsby loped along beside her to make sure she found her way, and I sat down on the stool behind the counter. I opened up the letter.

Dear Marianne,

One of my wishes for you is that you'll find good people who support your dreams. I found that in Corinne, who I talk so much about. She always said the saddest thing was a dream that went unwatered. And so she did her best to help us pursue the thing we wanted most.

I wish I could write a book about the magical blue house. At night, we'd build a fire out by the water, and Rob would tell ghost stories that he assured us held just a smattering of truth—so that we should always keep an ear out for noises in the night. And then kids swore they heard the ghost of an old sea captain who had lost his way pursuing some vast treasure. And some heard ghostly singing once we'd turned out the lights and cleaned up from our shows. I'd like to think that was true, at least. The sea captain? Not so much.

Oh, my Marianne, those were such fine days—the kind of days I hope you'll have as well. But it sadly didn't last. You see, there came a day when Corinne had to go. They said she did some things that I don't think were true. But the evil and the lies won out, as sometimes happens in the world.

Roger told me some about it. He was still in town, working at the bank. And it was at the bank that Roger saw some things he wished he hadn't seen. But he wouldn't talk about it. He wanted me to keep my good memories intact. He wanted the people who were heroes to stay that way in my mind.

And once you find those people who will support your dreams, I have one more wish for you, my daughter. I want you to BE that person for someone else's dream. Dream big—and pass it on.

I folded up the letter with a new to-do list forming in my mind.

1. *Figure out which bank Houston worked at.*
2. *Who is still around who might have been there with him?*

Elizabeth was right. If you look closely at the past, the present might make sense—if you just knew where to look.

CHAPTER THIRTEEN

Soon, Marianne was out the door with a book on the history of the Troubles in Northern Ireland, and I dashed back to Elizabeth's corner of the store. She was thumbing through a shoebox of old letters.

I was out of breath with my discovery. "Houston!" I handed her the letter. "He had some information on Corinne from all those years ago. And I think he had a plan to use that information to get something that he wanted. And that's why he was here."

Startled, she glanced down at the letter. "Oh, my goodness, Rue. What are you going on about?"

"Just read the letter and you'll see. It was brought in for your book."

She studied it and frowned. *"Working at the bank… I'd*

bet you anything it was Fordham Bank and Trust. It used to be there at the corner—you know, where Albert Baily has his fish shop."

"Oh, yeah. So I've heard." Albert loved to tell the tale of how the much-loved Jackie's Fish House had come into existence.

A sprightly man now in his eighties, he had been a loan officer at the venerable institution, which was still the go-to bank for the movers and the shakers here. It was now located closer into town. When the move had been announced, Albert had been dismayed. For one thing, he couldn't drive, and the original location was within easy walking distance from his sprawling home in the historic district. And on top of that, his friends had been begging him for years to open up a restaurant. One of the most sought-after invitations in Somerset Harbor had been an invitation to one of his garden parties. The pièce de résistance had been the delectable fish stew, the recipe for which was a closely guarded secret passed down by his mom.

So he had bought the building and stayed right there in place, cooking up an aromatic mixture of onions, sea bass, and tomatoes rather than cooking up business deals from behind the desk. "I should have done it sooner. Much more pleasant work," he'd said. He was a good-hearted man, and I could just imagine how much he had hated telling people "no" when they came in, hopeful, for a loan. Now, he could always tell them "yes" when they came in asking eagerly if they could get a bowl of the world's best stew.

"I think we're on to something." Elizabeth glanced around at her neat collections of ephemera. "Do you have some time to help me do some snooping?"

"Always," I told her. "I'll just listen for the bell."

Elizabeth stood up and put her hands on her hips. "Hmm. Let's see what I might have about the Fordham Bank." She handed me a large box. "Here. These are all business photos marked by decade. See what you can find. I'll go through the scrapbooks and see if I get a hit." She eyed a big stack of vintage scrapbooks stacked up in the corner. They were among her favorite finds when she set out for a day of sales, armed with water bottles and her best worn-in sneakers.

I would sneak back and read them on days when things were slow. I especially loved the ones with carefully pasted recipes from vintage magazines or handwritten by someone's great-great-aunt.

"Oh, did I tell you?" she said. "I'm going in on Tuesday for the TV interview. I hope I'll do okay."

"You'll be great," I said, pulling out a stack of photos to sit down with at the table. "Just put on a little lipstick, and you'll be absolutely charming—as you always are." I had absolutely no doubt that she would tell her story well. When something stirred her passions, it was hard for others not to get excited too. But this was television. A little makeup would be nice, and I knew that my best friend saw makeup as a bother.

"Oh, yes. You and your lipstick. As if a little dab of red will help me sell the story—or make a little bit of difference in the world."

I flipped through the photos, mostly black-and-whites, which dated back to the days far before my time in Somerset Harbor. I was surprised, however, that many of the buildings were the same—churches, lots of stores, and the magnificent Somerset Library, located in a former residence, complete with a big front porch for reading. (I really loved the place. Technically, I guessed, it was my competition. But perhaps some of the discoveries made among its hallowed stacks would send customers to me. They might want a sequel. Or more from a beloved author, copies of their own that they could mark up and keep.)

Then something caught my eye in a photograph; I recognized the logo of the Fordham Bank and Trust. There seemed to be a whole group of photos here that were taken at the bank. I flipped through photographs of men who were dressed in suits and shaking hands. Scanning the images, I was arrested by a photo of a pretty blonde in a business suit, smiling at the camera. It appeared as if she'd been taken by surprise by the presence of the person taking the photograph. *Wait a minute. Was that Allie?* Of course, it couldn't be. This was long before her time. But there were Allie's eyes; there was her mischievous grin. A coldness filled my chest at the stark reminder: she and I would never share a laugh again.

Across from me at the table, Elizabeth was flipping through a scrapbook. I slid the photo to her. "Catherine Lane?" I asked. "I swear it could be Allie! Don't you think?"

Elizabeth tilted her head as she studied the photograph. "Catherine or Corrinne. They looked so much alike."

"Oh, yeah. I'd forgotten they were twins."

"But that must be Catherine with the makeup and the suit, probably there on business for her father. You really never saw Corinne looking all that put together. She was more...*bohemian* I guess would be the word. Messy curls and flowy skirts, all those kinds of things."

"Not fit for a little outing to a bank? A lack of makeup did you say? As if a little dab of lipstick might make a bit of difference in how one is perceived?"

She waved away my teasing. "Yeah, yeah, yeah, I get it." She smiled down at the picture. "Yeah, this is Catherine, I think. But if it wasn't for the hair and the way they dressed, those two could have caused all kinds of confusion."

"Except for the clothes and hair—and the fact that they never spoke to one another and never even hung out with the same groups of people, which is really sad."

I flipped through more pictures and found Catherine in several, still wearing the same suit. Most likely, they were taken on the same day, I supposed. What exactly was the purpose of all these boring photos? They seemed to be so random—just groups of people lined up in formal poses or seemingly captured for all time in ordinary moments of talking to each other, staring down at stacks of papers, or talking on old-fashioned phones attached to curly cords.

Twice, the pretty blonde was pictured with two men. "Is that Albert?" I asked Elizabeth. He looked impossibly young. I handed her the picture.

"Yes, that would be our favorite fish chef," she said with a smile. "Hey, tomorrow we should go for lunch and take this picture to him. Ever since I said his name, I've been thinking of that stew. I haven't been in ages, and he'd really get a kick out of..." She paused to stare down at the photo. "Oh my goodness, I believe—"

I waited and waited. She did not complete the sentence.

"*What?* Elizabeth! What is it?"

She slid the photo back to me. "Who do you think that is?" she asked. "The other person in the picture…"

He looked to be in his early twenties, serious and handsome. *Something* about him looked familiar. "I have no clue," I said, finally giving up. "Some customer of ours?"

"Well, if he were scowling, you might have known him right away." She took the picture back and squinted at it. "At least, I *think* that's him."

"Roger Houston?"

"Maybe. There's something about the eyes…"

"Well, he did work at the bank—which is, after all, the reason we're going through this stuff. Interesting," I said. "We'll take this to Albert and see what he remembers." Would he recall anything at all about this seemingly very boring—and much-photographed—day at the bank and trust?

CHAPTER FOURTEEN

*T*he next afternoon found us enjoying our lunch at Jackie's Fish House where there was a special on pecan or apple pie, both of them freshly baked. The crowd by then had been cleared out long enough for Albert to sit with us and talk while we ate our lunch.

He had been delighted with the picture, although the contents also had made him melancholy. "Who'd have thought that of the three of us, it would be this old man who outlived the other two?" he asked.

He had indeed confirmed that the second man was Houston. "Just a shame what happened. I'd heard that he was back, and I really hoped he'd stop by and say hi. He was my assistant at the bank and trust for about a year. Polite and really sharp. I thought he was going places."

The aging chef leaned back and sighed, still studying the picture. "Of course, I heard all the talk. It seems that Roger Houston was not as...likable...as he was back in the day when he was my right-hand man. Life changes people sometimes. Life must have hit him hard."

"Do you remember that day? From the photograph?" I asked, dipping my spoon into the stew.

"Oh, yes. It was the only time I had the honor of meeting Catherine Lane. It was always Peter Carrington who came in to deal with us when it came to the family business. As big as the operations grew to be, he wanted to put *his* eye on things when it came to the money. But this was personal to Catherine. I remember well. And it just so happened a photographer was there. He was taking shots for an advertisement, if I remember right."

I swallowed a warm and buttery bite of my thick and yeasty roll. "I've heard that despite the family trouble, Catherine Lane was kind enough to throw a lifeline to her sister—and keep the café open."

He nodded and lowered his voice to a hushed tone. "Not that a banking man should speak of private things —confidential, don't you know? But that's why she'd come in." He picked up his coffee. "And to me, that marked the lady as a fine example of how a person should behave. I know she was under family pressure to turn her back on Corinne. But with all the money that the Carringtons pulled in, it would have been a shame for that café to close its doors."

It *would have.* I agreed. But by the time of this grand gesture, Corinne had delivered a low blow that would have prompted almost any sister to cut off all ties then and there. Something didn't fit.

"Did she talk to you about it?" I spooned up the last bit of my soup. "What made her decide that she'd step in to help?"

"Oh, she had a lot to say about the power that a place like that had to change the future. It used to be that kids would come here from all over to put on little shows right there in the café. And people came to hear them! Sometimes they'd get jobs to play in other places—or they might find mentors to help them along in their careers. I used to go and watch. It was quite a thing, I tell you."

"Too bad it had to change." Elizabeth stuck a fork into her pie.

"Yeah, that was a shame." Albert seemed to remember something then threw back his head and laughed. "Catherine was quite spirited that day. She was something else! I remember it so well. It's not often that you hear someone break out into song right there in the bank. Just a line or two, but she had quite the voice."

I glanced at Elizabeth. More and more, this little

scene seemed to be way off. From everything I'd heard, Catherine was the quiet and refined one while her twin, Corinne, was more full of life—the one you might expect to burst into song in the middle of a bank.

Houston had seen something at the bank that had shown him a darker side of his beloved mentor. I was now pretty sure I knew what that something was.

"And Roger Houston was a part of this joyous occasion!" I remarked as I picked up my fork and pulled my pie plate toward me.

"But I have to say the boy was acting really odd. It was the only time I saw him treat a customer with anything other than the most professional demeanor. He was assisting me when she made the withdrawal, and the look he gave that woman I never will forget."

"But why?" Elizabeth asked, confused.

"Wouldn't talk about it. To this day, I still don't know."

After finishing our desserts, we said our goodbyes to Albert and walked back toward the store. When we came to an alley between a dry cleaner and a deli, I pulled Elizabeth aside for some privacy. I didn't have the patience to wait until we reached our destination to see what she thought.

"Are you thinking what I'm thinking?" I asked in a low voice.

"Well, for some reason, Roger Houston was not a fan of Catherine—despite the fact the lady had come into the bank to save a business that supposedly he loved. Which I guess boosts the theory it was Houston who did away with Allie's mother—and maybe Allie too."

"I don't think that was Catherine who came into the bank. Catherine wouldn't sing out loud in a public place like that. Not from what I've heard. She was the proper twin—the shy one. But most of all, she was not the twin who would write that check—not after everything that went down with her sister."

Elizabeth turned white. "I think you're on to something. And then in comes Houston, who knew Corinne so well. Houston knew exactly what Corinne was doing!" She paused to think about it. "But he didn't say a word—because he believed in the café and its mission."

"Even if he'd stopped believing in Corrine." I took a calming breath. "Oh for the love of Dr. Seuss! This is some crazy stuff." I tried to fit this information in with all the other things we already knew. "So that's the little trump card that Houston had on Rob. That's why Rob was willing to go back to the old ways—with music over profit. If Houston were to speak up and take his story to the cops, that would be a lot of money, I suppose, that the Eighth Street Café would have to pay back somehow to Catherine Lane's estate."

"Which would have been a motive for him to poison Houston—who, after all, dropped dead right there in Rob's café." Elizabeth paused to think. "So, did he kill Allie too?"

"I don't know why he would—unless she also knew about what Corinne had done." I flipped through the mental files tucked away in my head until I came to ones labeled "Allie: Murder." Then I grabbed my friend's arm. "She did know! Allie knew. Andy said to me that she and Houston were seen talking not long before she died. He said Allie seemed upset. He must have told her then."

"And," said Elizabeth, "our waiter at the café told us Allie came into the business right about that time and had some words with Rob."

"Motive and opportunity: I believe we have them both. When we get back to the store, I'm calling Andy right away. I believe we solved the case!"

A sense of great relief settled in my chest, but I still had questions. Something still seemed off with Barry. And the weather girl! How was she involved?

Then like a coincidence that only comes in books, I caught a glimpse of Barry just ahead. It was as if the guy had been summoned by my thoughts! "Look who it is," I whispered. "Why is he still in town? I thought he had to get back."

"Very, very odd," said Elizabeth.

Barry darted into a pub, and I almost followed—but my need to get in touch with Andy overpowered my curiosity about Allie's fiancé.

"Things are busy here," Andy told me when I called.

"I will make it worth your while," I said.

"Oh, Rue, I don't know. The public's really pushing for us to solve this thing."

"Which I might have done. Get over here. Right now."

Once he had appeared and heard our story, Andy was amazed.

Albert had begged us for the photo, but we showed Andy all the others from the day that "Catherine Lane" had taken money from the bank.

"It absolutely fits," he said. "Rue, I'm flabbergasted." With his hands on his hips, he blew out a stream of air. "We will need you both to come into the station and make official statements, and we'll talk to Albert too. I'll need to have that picture that is now in his possession. But I'm thinking we'll be able to wrap this thing up pretty quick—thanks to our ace detectives. You girls were excellent."

I nodded, my pleasure tinged with melancholy; there was no victory, after all, that could bring back Allie.

"Okay, will you tell me some things now?" I asked. "Because I think you owe me, Andy. Why were you so sure that Allie's murder was related to the candy business?"

"I can't go into detail. But Something Sweet, to be quite frank, had some business practices that were on the sour side," he said. "There was a whole long list of people who were out to get revenge. And as for Roger Houston, early on we got a tip that he was going on and on to someone about the crooked Carringtons—and something or other to do with a bank. And now I guess we know what that was all about."

Since my helper Ellen was due at any minute, we told Andy that we'd stop in at the station later in the afternoon.

"You're a smart one, Rue," he said. "Thanks to your good work, your old buddy Andy might just get back soon to his old sweet life—afternoon naps and all." He touched me on the shoulder. "You did good for Allie."

"et's take a detour," I said, as we walked out the door about twenty minutes later, heading to the station. "Let's stop by at the pub."

Elizabeth's eyes went wide. "Are you serious? The pub? It's early for a drink, and don't you imagine, Rue, that they need our statements now?"

"They need our smarts is what they need," I told her in a low voice, "and there are still unanswered questions —things that just don't add up. I want to see what Barry's up to if he's still in that pub."

"Well, that does make sense, I guess."

Inside, the pub was dimly lit and most of the booths and tables were unoccupied. Three ladies talked loudly around a table that was littered with dirty cups and napkins, while an older couple sat quietly in a booth nearby.

But there was no Barry.

The girl behind the bar caught my eye and waved. I recognized her as a fan of young-adult fantasies. Barry or no Barry, I guessed we should go in. It would seem rather odd to simply, well, just *leave* after standing in the entrance for two minutes.

We sat down at the bar and ordered virgin daiquiris. Champagne would come a little later when the killer was locked up behind bars.

"How did you like that last book?" I asked the girl as she made our drinks. I remembered now that her name was Hannah.

"Double awesome," she said. "I read it in one day." She looked around the room. "Because as you can see, you have a lot of time to read here if you work afternoons."

"Well, come on back," I said, "and we can load you up."

Some movement caught my eye in a darkened corner of the bar. A couple in the back was pressed together kissing, and it did not appear as if they'd come up for air real soon.

"People, get a room." Elizabeth picked up her drink.

I shrugged. Who were they hurting? I was a little

jealous if you want the honest truth. I loved Somerset Harbor, and I loved the life I'd made, but all the male customers who came in seemed to be teenagers or old men.

"I would never have predicted they'd end up in that… position…when that guy first walked in," Hannah whispered to us. "He was *not* too glad to see her. It was quite the argument!"

Interesting, I thought. "What was the fight about?"

"Rue!" Elizabeth touched my hand. "That is not our business." Then she looked at Hannah. "Although I'd really like to know." She smiled.

"They were being kind of quiet. It was more the tone that let me know that things were getting tense." Hannah wiped the counter. "But I heard *we can be together now* and *please leave me alone* and *never, ever have been able to get over you.*" She shrugged. "So who really knows?"

I tried to down my drink fairly quickly because this did not seem right: drinking in a pub while the cops were anxiously waiting down the street to take our statements. I was reaching for my purse to pay when the couple from the back walked past us, hand in hand. When I turned to look, I was face to face with a wide-eyed Barry.

I watched his face turn white. Then he put his head down and rushed out.

I turned to the girl.

It was Regina Whatley, who was blushing. "Oh my!" she said. "Well, this is…well, hello! You girls enjoy your drinks." Then she rushed out as well.

I glanced at Elizabeth. It seemed there was no shortage of suspects who had motives.

At the station, things were busy. Andy introduced Elizabeth to an Officer Susan Bright, who took her back to give her statement.

"Follow me," he said. "I'll take you back to meet Bill Simpkins, who'll get your statement from you. It shouldn't take too long."

"But Andy, just a minute. Rob might not be the person who killed Allie."

"What? Rue, of course he is. You're the one who came to me with all the evidence! He clearly had a reason to want Roger Houston gone, and then the guy falls over dead right there at Rob's café, which makes it almost certain that he killed Allie too. Allie also died by poison, and we have reason to believe that she had been made aware of incriminating evidence that could send our guy Rob to prison. Or, at the very least, force him to change things at his business in a way that means a lot less money in his pocket." He looked down at the floor. "Of course, we aren't certain that he was aware of what Corinne was up to, but the woman was his partner. We'll bring him in today and if all goes well, we are hoping the man will just confess. It surely would be nice to avoid a trial on this one."

"But I'm thinking now that Barry might have—" I found myself choked up. It was all too awful. I almost couldn't say it. "I'm wondering now if Barry might have been the one to hurt her."

Andy simply stared. "Rue, what in the world? You're the one who came to me with evidence that it was someone else!" He sighed. "You've become a friend—one of my best friends, really. But this is exasperating. You can be so confusing!"

"You see, we were in the pub just now—"

"Before you came in for your statement, you stopped at *the pub*?"

"Please! Let me explain." I told him the story.

"Well, well, well." He was very quiet as he took it in. "We'd heard Barry was a ladies' man, and that gave us pause—like perhaps the guy just wasn't ready to up and settle down. It's not unheard of as a motive. In fact, it's way too common. Which is why this job can make you lose your faith in people."

"But it could be Rob as well! Oh, Andy, I don't know."

"Well, the good thing, Rue, is that you don't *have* to know. Just tell your story to the experts, and we will find a way—I hope—to put the pieces all together." He sighed. "I will let Officer Simpkins know your statement will be more extensive than we at first believed." He put his hand on my shoulder. "We will get whoever did this. Don't you worry, Rue."

CHAPTER SIXTEEN

*T*he next day at noon, Andy called my cell as I was dusting shelves in the section for biographies and history.

"I have news," he said. "I wanted you to know that we talked to Rob, and the guy confessed. But Rue, you won't believe which murder he confessed to."

"So he did not confess to both?" I was kind of expecting that it would be both or neither.

"He confessed to killing *Catherine* all those years ago!"

Catherine. Of course. The first murder in the series had almost slipped my mind. Of course, it made a lot of sense that he'd killed Allie's mom as well—with help from Corinne? But I felt certain Catherine's twin would have gone that far. She had crossed some lines, to say the least, in the name of a good cause, but I didn't think she would have killed her sister.

"But out of the three murders, he just confessed to one?" Now, I was confused.

Andy cleared his throat. "Here's where it gets weird. This guy is *insisting* that it wasn't him who killed the other two. He said he's tortured all the time by what he did to Catherine all those years ago, and no way would he even dream of doing that again."

Did that mean it was Barry? I sat down in shock on a nearby stool. "Do you believe him, Andy?"

"Actually, I do. I sat in on the interview, and I think it was the truth. He readily confessed to the older crime. It was like the guy was tired and just wanted to let go of that heavy burden and put it out there on the table. That's sometimes the way it goes. But when that is the case, they tell you everything. They don't confess to one crime and lie about the others."

"Wow. So he killed *Allie's mother.*"

"Yeah," Andy said and then went further into the details. Apparently, Rob also had admitted that he had been aware of Corinne's deception when she posed as her sister to get funds for their business. As soon as the funds went missing, Catherine understood where the money had gone and how the funds had made it from her bank account to the coffers of the Eighth Street

Café. Rob immediately had grown nervous after that, but Corinne had reassured him that everything was fine; Catherine wouldn't tell. Because while Catherine had no love for her sister anymore, she did like the idea of the café staying open. In fact, the teenage daughter of Catherine's cleaning lady was a singer on the Eighth Street stage and could not stop her enthusiastic gushing about the program there.

After the incident, Catherine had paid a visit to the café to let her sister know that she was onto her. Rob had been present for the meeting, so he always knew at least one person in the world could testify that both business owners were in on the crime.

They went on like that for several years, with him feeling fairly certain that Catherine would keep their secret safe. After all, an arrest in the case would bring shame upon the family.

Then somehow rumors started that there was something not quite right going on at the café. Had Catherine let something slip to someone? Or maybe all the talk was not connected to the loan at all. It could've just been grousing by a disgruntled former worker or perhaps a business owner who competed with the café for the same kinds of customers. He never really knew, and then the rumors died down with no specific accusations.

But during those nervous several months, he feared the gig was up, and so did Corinne.

Reluctantly, Corinne left for another city. It was her plan and Rob's that if anyone showed up with any official accusations, he simply would deny any understanding that the money had been stolen. He could feign shock and disbelief and pretend to be disgusted at what his former partner had done to get the money.

But of course, there was one person left in town who could say that was all wrong. With rumors flying all over Somerset Harbor, Rob made the decision to get rid of that person. Being a person who was good at the kitchen arts, he came up with what he deemed to be a perfect plan. He made a single piece of candy—a dark chocolate raspberry truffle, which he sprinkled liberally with peanuts and with poison. Then he mailed the thing to Catherine in care of Something Sweet. In a childish scrawl, he had written her a letter that supposedly had come from a ten-year-old superfan of Something Sweet Confections. "I dream of chocolate making too, and I've made this for you. I hope you think it's good, and I can be like you one day."

As Andy told the story of the murderous confession, I gazed out the window, watching people gathering in groups and rushing to appointments. Word had gotten out that there was movement in the case; news travels fairly quickly here.

"Have you talked to Barry?" I asked Andy.

"He's gone MIA. If he's in any of the local inns, it's not under his real name. We sent a car by Regina Whatley's, but there was no sign of him there."

Very weird, I thought as a customer walked in. "Gotta go," I said. "Let me know if there are updates, and I'll see you at home. Want me to stop by Melba's and pick us up some chowder?"

"Excellent," he said. "You are a good one, Rue. Bringing in a killer and bringing me hot soup, all in a few days' time. Way to multi-task."

Although the town felt safe, Andy still was in the guest room. I expected he would leave once the case was wrapped, but for now we both enjoyed a little company when we got in from work.

I helped the customer, a young girl, pick out some romances. Then the bell rang again.

I looked up and saw Ellen walking in to begin her shift. She gave me a little wave. Noticing a new box behind the counter, she began to shelve the new arrivals on the bestseller table. Then she headed to the counter when she saw our customer was ready to check out.

I went back to my dusting, and my mind returned to

Barry. Was he staying at Regina's or had he gone back home after our encounter at the bar?

Elizabeth breezed past me, wearing nice black slacks and a colorful silk blouse. "Do I look camera-ready? Oh, Rue, I'm so afraid that when they get that mic out, I'll forget my name."

"You look beautiful," I said, "and I'm there for you if you need a ride-along. Moral support and all!" Plus, perhaps, a chance to have a little chat with the local weather girl, speaking of people in this town with a reason to be nervous. That might give me a better sense of how likely it really was that Barry was the killer.

I glanced toward Ellen, who gave me a nod to signal she was good with me leaving for a while. The store was very quiet.

"That would be fantastic." Elizabeth took a deep breath. "Let's go and do this thing."

CHAPTER SEVENTEEN

*a*fter my best friend was swept into the back by a producer, I waited in the Channel 8 lobby. I picked up the scent of coffee coming from a closed door to my left. Was that the employee break room? That would be my best bet to run into Regina.

I glanced toward the receptionist, who seemed to be the type who kept a close eye on all the doors. I supposed she'd seen her share of overeager fans wanting to get close to the anchors and reporters who were the closest thing we had here to celebrities.

"Employees Only," warned a sign on the door. I breathed in the coffee and seemed to get a boost just from the rich aroma. They bought the good stuff, I supposed.

Then I heard a familiar voice from behind the door.

"It will be good news from me," I heard Regina say. "Sunshine all week long."

I needed to be in there.

I wandered toward reception and smiled warmly at the young girl working behind the desk. "I hate to disturb you, but is there anywhere at all that I could get a cup of coffee while I wait for my friend?"

The girl shook her head. "Oh, ma'am, I'm so sorry, but we don't have any kind of café for the public, just a break room for the staff."

"Oh, I understand." I put my head to my forehead. "I assumed that was the case. It's just that I've had this headache that will not go away."

She gave me a sad smile. "My mother gets those too, and she does say caffeine helps."

I looked down at the desk and saw a book on a stack of papers next to the girl's computer. *Friendships and Betrayals.*

Hmm. Show me what a person's reading, and I can make a good guess about how to bond with them. But I had to hurry. It would not take Regina long to pour a cup of coffee for herself and get out of there.

I made myself wince again. "This one is a migraine, which I tend to get when I'm really stressed. You see, my best friend in the world, who was almost like my sister...at least I *thought* she was my friend...oh, would you listen to me? Just going on and on. And I know you must be busy! I do apologize. It's just been the saddest day." I rubbed my head again and gave her my best version of a brave, determined smile.

"Oh, you poor, poor thing!" she said, then she lowered her voice to a whisper. "You would not believe it, but something *very* similar has absolutely *rocked my world.* You just slip into that door right there and get yourself some coffee." She nodded toward the break room. "Oh, and hon, I do hope you feel better really soon."

"Thank you so, so much," I said as I headed for the break room.

Luckily, Regina was still by the coffee pot, talking to a man. She looked shocked to see me. "Oh!" Her face turned red.

"How are you, Regina?" I reached for a cup. "I've come in with Elizabeth. She's being interviewed right now for the letters project." I put my hand on her arm. "Thank you so much for your help."

"Oh! I'm just glad it worked out. Really awesome project. Really glad to help." She looked down at the floor. Heavy in the silence was the memory of our meeting at the pub. By that point, the man had slipped out, and she and I were alone.

"You must think I'm awful," she whispered in a voice that I could barely hear.

Now that I was with her face to face, I had no idea how to even start to fish for info. But flush with my new success in bonding via common traumas, I had an idea.

"I don't judge," I said. "If I see a happy couple, I'm just thankful that they've somehow found each other in the world. I kind of stink at love. I could be the poster girl, I guess, for bad romance. Except there was this one guy." I gave her a small smile. "This one guy, he was perfect. Except one day, he bought a ring—and it was not for me. And that just broke my heart."

"You see, that's the thing!" she said. "I know how it must have looked, right after Allie's death. But I go way back with Barry; what we had was real. In fact, when he met Allie, he had come to town to visit me. You see, loved me first—until they met on the street. And one day, he told me he was sorry, but that love had hit him hard. He was obsessed with Allie!"

"That was my story too." I let my eyes grow wide. Perhaps I should try my hand at writing. I was good at spinning tales.

Regina looked down at her coffee. "I tried everything I could to let him know I was the one—not her. I really love him, Rue, and I think we're meant to be. But he wouldn't see me, and I guess that was for the best." She frowned. "Oh, the look in that man's eyes when he said Allie's name! That almost killed me, Rue. It was Allie that he loved. He tried to tell me all along, but I didn't want to listen."

"Well, that kind of thing is hard," I said sympathetically.

"I did some foolish things, Rue. And now I'm so embarrassed. I would even make things up to get him to come to me. I'd say I'd sprained an ankle and that I needed food. I even made a story up about getting mugged."

Okay, the girl was nuts. Had *she* been the one to go after Allie?

"But then things began to happen." She took a sip of coffee. "Oh, I really need to go. My producer will be frantic."

"But tell me, please. What happened?"

"Roger Houston came by here, and he was all upset. He was upset about some things at that Eighth Street Café. He used to be there with my mother when they were both young kids. The place was very different than it is today. Because my mom was there, he thought I could do a story. I tried to tell him that I'd do what I could to help. But I do the weather! Plus, he didn't seem to have the kind of proof we'd need to put it on the news. But he was insistent. The guy was so intense!" Then her eyes grew wide. "After that, things happened really fast. Allie died, and Roger died. And I knew from Roger that there were connections there— between Allie's family and the café owner that he'd come here to confront. So, when both of them were poisoned, I figured, hey, that's why—so that they wouldn't tell. Because Allie knew as well about the bad stuff that was supposedly going on. Roger had told Allie, and she was so upset! So I went to Barry to tell him what I knew."

"That's some heavy stuff," I said. Of course, I'd already known about all of those connections. But something nagged at me. Why had Barry never given any of that info to the cops? Perhaps he thought she'd made it up—like the mugging and the injured ankle.

Regina sighed. "I tried my best to give him comfort in my own special way, to let him know that it was not too late to get back what we lost. But he wasn't having it —at least until last night. But Rue, it still feels wrong— like I'm second best. He was staying with me at my house, but he left first thing this morning. He's not over Allie. I don't think he ever will be, even though she's gone."

On behalf of Allie, I felt a sense of gratefulness. She had been truly loved. But if Barry hadn't killed her, and Rob was innocent, who had slipped a dose of poison to my friend? Was I having coffee with the murderer right now?

"Well, I really have to run. Thanks for listening, Rue." Regina rushed off to her work, and I headed to the lobby, where Elizabeth was waiting.

She gave me a thumbs-up. "The interview went great," she said. "They made it comfortable, like I was talking to a friend and not a zillion people out there in TV Land."

"I'm so glad," I said. I turned to my new friend at the reception counter. "Thank you so much," I mouthed.

She smiled. "Chin up and stay strong! Just do what I'm doing and pick a better class of friends."

Elizabeth looked at me, confused. "Did I do something wrong?"

I took her arm and led her toward the door so I could explain outside.

CHAPTER EIGHTEEN

I was feeling restless when we got back to work. With the store still quiet, I left things in the hands of Elizabeth and Ellen. I needed space to think and to quiet all the questions scrolling through my head.

I found myself at the far end of the parking lot of the Eighth Street Café, watching the comings and goings from the building, which was quiet now between the lunch and dinner hours. I sipped some tea from a to-go cup as I watched a bluebird fly onto a branch of an old oak tree. I thought of the little crystal bird that Allie had brought into the store not long before she'd died. She had found it, I remembered, among her mother's things. *She always told me, "Allie, when you see a bluebird, that means things will be okay."* Perhaps this was a sign from Catherine that we were getting close.

I sent a text to Andy. *Barry's gone back home.*

I got an answer right away. *How do you know that?*

I had a little heart-to-heart today with Regina Whatley. Barry didn't do it. He was still in love with Allie.

We'll still send someone out to try to talk to him.

I watched as the bird ruffled its bright feathers. It matched the color of the house, where an older couple was exiting onto the porch. This had been a special place once. Perhaps it could be again. There were changes planned. But now with Rob in jail, who knew what the future held?

Anxious to wrap up this case for Allie, I tried to think of who—other than the café owner—might want her and Houston dead. Regina had a motive to kill Allie, but would she kill Houston too? And why?

At that point, Adriana got out of a car with a friend, their eyes glued to their phones. Adriana nonchalantly tossed her hair over her shoulder and pulled two shopping bags from the back seat of the friend's red Mercedes. I recognized the name on one of the bags, although it was not a store where I could afford to shop. And the thing about it was, neither could Adriana.

And that is when it hit me. Right here was a girl

whose fondest wishes would come true if the café could just hold on to its money-making ways.

I thought back to the day that Roger Houston died. When she was not ignoring me and Elizabeth and our growling stomachs, Adriana was ignoring Houston, who was sitting at a table with Regina. I closed my eyes and tried to remember every little detail of the scene that day. Book people, don't you know, are really good at that. Our memories play out in our minds, complete with facial expressions, background noises, and the smells in the room.

Houston had barked at her for coffee, which she had delivered with a roll of her eye. And had there maybe been something else that was hiding in the girl's expression? Had there also been a gleam of triumph in her eye? I thought perhaps there was.

My heart began to race. She could have also poisoned Allie! Allie had been at the café not long before she died—and she'd become upset as she talked to Rob. Adriana could have overheard. She would have realized that Allie knew the secret that could force an unwanted change in her father's livelihood. And killing her would have been as easy as serving up a poisoned cup of coffee or perhaps dessert.

I picked up my phone and texted Andy once again. *Have you looked at the daughter—Adriana?*

Three minutes later, my phone buzzed and I picked it up.

"Why didn't I think of that?" he asked. "That just makes too much sense."

"Right? Who knows what that girl might do to keep herself decked out in Ralph Lauren and Hermes?" Suddenly I found myself near tears. "And that selfish little twit might have poisoned Allie, and for what? Another stupid pair of shoes. Andy, it's disgusting."

He was all business now. "We'll go back through our witnesses and see if anybody saw her pass some food or drink to one of the victims."

"You're speaking to one now."

A long silence followed that.

"Excuse me. Rue? What was that you said?"

I caught my breath. "I can't believe it, Andy. I might have seen it for myself: the moment that girl murdered Houston. I saw Adriana hand a cup of coffee over to him right before he died."

Andy was breathing hard. "I think you're on to something. Well, I've got to run. It seems as if we might have a case here that's about to break wide open."

CHAPTER NINETEEN

hree days later, the sun was setting on my front porch as I clinked my glass of champagne to Andy's. Adriana was in jail, having confessed quickly to the murders in a flood of tears once she understood that the police had pegged her as a suspect.

Andy shook his head. "Like father, like daughter, I suppose. Except for the fact that he has the decency at least to regret the thing he did."

"And all she regrets, I guess, is that she got caught. And that her prison orange is clashing in a most unattractive way with her designer shoes."

She had used rat poison, which was kept locked up in the back of the café. She'd kept small doses in baggies in her pocket, waiting for the right time to slip the stuff into the victims' food or drink.

"I'm just glad it wasn't Barry." I savored my champagne while I watched a line of pink sink into the oranges of the fading sun.

Beside me, Gatsby barked as if he agreed.

Andy rocked back in his chair. "If he had told us all that stuff that he'd heard from Regina, we'd have looked right away at Rob—although maybe not his daughter. But that's how it goes sometimes. Even when they've lost someone that they dearly love, people are so careful of what they say to cops."

Barry, it turned out, had been afraid to say too much about his contact with Regina, afraid that he'd look guilty. No fiancé of a dead girl wants to volunteer that he's been hanging with his ex. If the cops had asked around, they might have heard some stories about his encounters with Regina when he'd come to town. She would not leave him alone!

Barry had been hearing whispers about the way that most of the cops here were not the brightest bulbs. The easy path for them might be to pin the crime on him. He'd explained it all to Andy, who had been the one to wrap things up with Barry in a final interview.

Plus, Barry had assumed the stories from Regina were just more of her lies designed to make him want to talk to her. But just to check things out, he'd spent time at the café, studying the scene.

"And the sad thing is that he was right about the way the cops are in this town." Andy reached down toward his lap to pet the sleeping cat. "They might very well have gone after Barry if we knew about Regina. That might have blinded some of them to any other suspects."

"If not for you," I said. "You wouldn't let them do that. That's why you can't retire."

"Oh, I don't think the bad guys will get away with much as long as a certain seller of fine books is on the case."

"The same amateur that you accuse of interfering?" I gave him a teasing smile. "And I told you all along that they were connected—her death and her mother's." I took another sip of champagne and looked over at my friend. "I want to hear you say it."

He raised an eyebrow at me.

"Say it: I was right."

Andy smiled and nodded. A half-nod and a half-smile, but I'd take what I could get. The next morning he would leave to go back to his home, and I would miss our talks on the porch at night.

As the light began to fade more, I felt melancholy, like I often did at night. No amount of sleuthing could give Allie back her life—or bring Roger Houston back to see the music being brought back to the Eighth Street Café.

In the next few months, things were set to change at the restaurant: live music, a new menu. Applications had been sent out to colleges and high schools in the local area. A picnic and celebration had been planned to mark the change. Someone had donated money for a new coat of blue paint. Something new and hopeful, brought to us by a man who was filled with anger but also good intentions. Somewhere, maybe he was smiling. It might be the first time in a long, long time.

Plans had been put in place before Houston died. With Houston's death, the threat to Rob had lessened if not disappeared. But the employees were excited about the changes that were planned. So Rob had kept the plans in place. And now with Rob locked up, a manager would oversee the transformation.

"Hey, Rue, are you okay?" Andy was looking at me, worried.

I looked up toward the trees and caught sight of another bluebird that flew a little closer, landing on a nearby branch. The small bird seemed to glance at me before it flew away.

"Yeah, I think I will be fine. Something tells me, Andy, that things will be okay."

# # #

Thank you for reading! Want to help out?

Reviews are a crucial for independent authors like me, so if you enjoyed my book, **please consider leaving a review today**.

Thank you!

Penny Brooke

ABOUT THE AUTHOR

Penny Brooke has been reading mysteries for as long as she can remember. When not penning her own stories, she enjoys spending time outdoors with her husband, crocheting, and cozying up with her pups and a good novel. To find out more about her books, visit www.pennybrooke.com

Printed in Great Britain
by Amazon

81491345R00092